Inborn Error

A Novel

Bruce R. Gilbert

ISBN: 0692907645
ISBN 13: 9780692907641

Library of Congress Control Number: 2017917895
Russell Group LLC, Great Neck, NY

TABLE OF CONTENTS

Like many of life's adventures, writing a novel is a journey involving highs and lows, clarity and confusion, yet always a labor of love. My wife and best friend, Betsy, has been the most supportive and loving partner through the late nights and endless weekends involved in this journey. She has critiqued many versions of the manuscript. She is and has always been the love of my life and my source of inspiration.

ACKNOWLEDGMENTS

Writing a first novel, like being a first-time parent, has an exponential learning curve. I am so appreciative of my colleagues, friends, and family, who have offered practical advice and continual encouragement. Over a decade ago, I attended a medical fiction-writing weekend seminar for physicians, run by two exceptional authors and mentors: Michael Palmer and Tess Gerritsen. Their love of writing was contagious. I am incredibly grateful for their teaching and guidance. At their seminar, I met Rebecca Campen and David Trock. All three of us had a passion for writing and had novels at various stages of completion. We formed a writers' group, sending and critiquing chapters of one another's work at regular intervals. This process and their constructive comments and enthusiasm were invaluable.

INBORN (in´bōrn)
Inherited, present from birth.

ERROR (er´ōr)
A deficiency or imperfection in structure or function.

Webster's New Collegiate Dictionary, G.&C. Merriam Co., 1949

1

REFLECTIONS

Thursday, August 3, 1995

I had turned off the office lights and was about to close the door when I realized I had forgotten to take Bob Ludlow's chart and our research files home to review. I had sent out samples for evaluation, just to be sure, and data had arrived by courier this afternoon. With a full day of patients, I simply had no time to look at them. Bob and I were to meet the next morning with his attorney to discuss our patent ideas. We were under a deadline to file the patent. I needed to review this new data before the meeting. I needed to make sure I didn't overlook anything.

I reentered my office and picked up my briefcase from the floor next to my desk. I loved that briefcase. A dark-brown brushed-leather bag with a flap that allowed the handle to protrude. The flap had my name, "Barry Gifford, MD," imprinted in gold block lettering over the clasp. My wife, Linda, had given me the briefcase when I completed my fellowship. That was just two weeks before I proposed to her.

It was always so serene after hours. My staff left after the last patient was seen. Only the cleaning crew remained in the building. It was 10:00 p.m. Later than I usually leave the office on a Thursday. I had an unusual amount of chart notes to write and patient calls to return. Linda had already called twice to see what was keeping me. She was hoping I could be home to help with Justin and Diana. The kids were off from school that day because of a teacher conference, and she was with them all day. She needed a break. Each time she called, I had a pang of guilt. Don't get me wrong. I love what I do. Helping patients have families is so gratifying. I just feel these late hours are taking a toll on Linda and the kids. She doesn't say anything about it. But I feel it. Probably my conscience kicking in. I know I need to make a change. I just don't know how.

The research data was in a thin, sealed envelope and easily fit in my briefcase. Bob's chart was a fat file, containing the many tests Dr. Brunswick had ordered and surgery he had performed. It wouldn't fit in my briefcase, so I found that by clutching it under my left arm with my briefcase hanging from my left hand, I could use my right hand to lock the office door.

I took the elevator down to the first floor. I was hoping the back door to the parking lot was still open. I really didn't want to walk around the building to the parking lot. Fortunately, the back door was unlocked. I assumed my car was the last one in the lot. It usually was.

The parking lot was dark and quiet, the faint moonlight doing little to illuminate it. The building itself blocked the light as did the towering sycamore trees. The falling grayish-brown bark from the sycamores continually created headaches for the grounds crew. It was a warm August evening. There were only two lights in the parking lot. One near the back door and the other on the building. The latter, positioned in a landscaped area adjacent to the building, illuminated the free-standing sign that identified the building. I'd spoken many times to the landlord, Frank Carlton, about adding more lights so that it wasn't so dark when we were leaving the building after nine o'clock. Frank was an honest man—a self-made millionaire—but he was tightfisted. Never would he spend money on what he felt were "unnecessary expenses." Because I was the only tenant with evening office hours, he couldn't justify the expense—especially since we were in the best part of town, and there were no regulations requiring these lights.

As I approached my car, I heard a crunch from someone stepping on the sycamore bark. It appeared that it was coming from behind me. I turned in the direction of the sound and was enveloped by an explosive bright light. The pressure in my head was unbearable. Sounds became muffled, and my surroundings unclear. I could not feel the ground as I fell. A woman and a man were yelling at each other. I felt piercing pain as if I had been stabbed by an ice pick. The last thing I remembered before losing consciousness was the woman saying, "The chart, not the briefcase."

2

BEGINNINGS

Friday, September 16, 1955

The air was still, and the bright lights were reflecting off the glossy white walls and linoleum floor. Sounds of clanking instruments echoed from these cold surfaces as the nurses set up instruments for the delivery. The mother was told to expect twins. Her doctor had heard two heartbeats. The mother was hoping for her husband to be there with her. The rotary telephone on the table next to the bed had not rung. With every contraction, her knuckles whitened as she grasped the rails of the gurney. Beads of sweat coalesced into droplets that were now soaking her bedding. She did not want to scream, but somehow sounds found their way out.

The warmth and security of the womb was soon to be transformed into a battle for survival. The newly formed muscles were recruited into the crusade. The lungs, normally filled with amniotic fluid during intrauterine development, now needed to be emptied and replaced with life-sustaining air. Precious seconds remained for life to continue. The miracle of life? Seemed more like survival of the fittest. But the battle had just begun. If birth was a challenge, life would be an ordeal.

The father was not yet at the hospital. He had been called to another urgent meeting. He was always working. He had thought for sure the babies would not be ready to make their way into this world so quickly. He obviously didn't believe his wife when she said she couldn't go another day. Mothers, even first-time mothers, somehow have a sense about these things.

The marvel of birth: a baby is born, perfect in every way. An unqualified bond forms between mother and child. It wasn't going to be like that on this cold, damp Friday morning in September.

A cry filled the room as the first of the newborns completed the journey. The nurse stated the time and date of birth, so her assistant could record it: "Baby One delivered, seven oh five p.m., male child."

For the baby, the warmth and security of the womb were traded for the cold sterility of the delivery room, bringing with it an impassioned cry from the newborn and tears of joy from the new mother's eyes.

The activity of the delivery room was frenetic. The first of two teams was evaluating the firstborn and calculating the Apgar score, which Dr. Virginia Apgar at Columbia University had introduced in 1952. This simple measure was used to evaluate the newborn at one minute after birth. A perfect score of ten was almost never seen; however, a score less than three might indicate long-term neurologic damage. This baby boy was seven pounds, eight ounces, and nineteen inches long. He had a one-minute Apgar of nine, an almost perfect score. Pulse was 120. He had a loud cry and active movement of the extremities. He let out an even louder cry in response to the needle prick for the standard newborn blood tests. The Apgar lost a point for some bluish tinge in the extremities, but that was sure to clear.

The second child was making its way through the passageway when all contractions stopped. Five seconds, then ten seconds went by. All in the room became silent.

"Doctor," the nurse asked, her voice trembling a bit. "What should we do?"

"Just give it time," the venerable doctor replied. "They do it in their own time."

And as if on cue, a last contraction forced the head to pass the final centimeters. A weak cry was heard at first. Then as air filled the newly awakened lungs, the cry continued to gain strength, followed by a rapid change in skin color from a bluish tinge to the normal pink color. This child did not look normal. Was it a boy, or was it a girl? That would need to be addressed later. Too much was happening now. The nurse then stated so all could hear and so it could be recorded, "Baby Two delivered, seven twenty-five p.m., gender undetermined."

It was with obvious relief that the nurse from the second team took the baby to be cleaned, weighed, and swaddled. The Apgar was a bit lower, losing points for color, heart rate, and activity, but still a respectable seven. However, all was not complete. The afterbirth needed to be delivered and the mother checked on. With the contractions now back and rapidly increasing in frequency, this was sure to be soon.

The mother stopped sweating. Her face became pale. "Doctor, I'm feeling a bit dizzy, and I feel my heart pounding. Is that normal?"

However, the doctor already knew that all was not as it should be. The nurse took the mother's blood pressure, which was extremely low. Her pulse was very rapid. He knew she was losing blood. He examined her. His brow furrowed, and his face flushed as his gloved hands returned from the birth canal, soaked with blood.

"Blood pressure is a bit low, but we'll take care of that quickly." The doctor turned to the nurse and spoke softly so the mother would not hear. "Please get a unit of blood and hang it stat. Make sure two more are in the room. And call Dr. Morgen. Get him here right away. We also need a third team. We've got another one coming, and the mother is bleeding internally."

As if a switch was flipped, the previously frenetic atmosphere slowed and became organized. Like a well-trained pilot handling an emergency, the team began a well-rehearsed protocol. A new urgent agenda was in play. The outcome was uncertain.

"Doctor," the patient said, while the doctor moved closer to hear her better, "why are the lights getting so dark?" Her voice continued to lose strength. "Why do I feel so cold?" As these last words left the new mother's pursed lips, her eyes closed, and her once anxious facial mask was replaced by one of peacefulness.

"I'm losing her!" the previously unflappable doctor shouted. "Let's get the blood hung now and prepare for an emergency C-section—now!" He shouted again as if his words themselves would cause action. "And call a code!" The ominous red bell on the wall started ringing.

The bleeding needed to be stopped if the mother was to survive. The doctor quickly made a vertical incision downward from the umbilicus. The uterine walls were too thin and had ruptured during the birth of the first two children. Blood cascaded out of the uterus and filled the pelvis. The third baby was delivered just as the new team arrived. The baby appeared lifeless. An Apgar of three. This baby was blue. The umbilical cord was cut. The baby was passed to the third team's nurse. The placentas were rapidly delivered. The doctor packed surgical lab pads into the uterus to try to clear the blood and find where the bleeding was coming from. But as soon as a lap pad was placed, it was soaked by the blood. The uterus was unsalvageable. The doctor decided to remove the uterus. But it was too late. The bleeding couldn't be controlled. Too much blood was lost. Blood pressure crashed. The monitors flatlined. The mother would never again hear her babies' cries. The nurse, usually so responsive to stating the time and date of birth, was too distraught. She cradled the baby in her arms and began sobbing. An instant bond was formed almost as if she were the birth mother. The time and date of birth and gender were never reported for this third child.

The father was arriving as his wife was being wheeled to the morgue. Two of the babies had been placed in separate bassinets. They looked at each other as they were wheeled to the nursery, as if they knew that no distance could separate them. The third baby was still being resuscitated by the team. Some say that a special connection, a paranormal bond, exists among triplets. They seemed to sense the fears and pain of one another even if separated by distance. The first two babies began crying. The third sibling was struggling to survive. The father sat expressionless on a chair in the now quiet delivery room. One single tear fell from his right eye. The wind was howling as the rain somberly pelted the rippled-glass windowpanes.

3

INTOLERANCE

Friday, September 16, 1955

The rain continued falling as the father, Robert Ludlow, arrived at his sprawling Tudor mansion, which he fondly called the castle. He was master of his castle and the empire he built. His staff, and many of his colleagues, out of respect, called him the governor. The house was perched on a knoll and surrounded by elegant oak trees. It was a breathtaking location thirty miles north of Stamford, Connecticut. Some of the leaves had started to turn golden, while acorns already lay on the ground. It was mid-September, and in only a few weeks the leaves would be falling. This gave the staff much work since the governor insisted that the grounds be perfectly manicured. Not even a lone acorn could be left on the stone paths. His intolerance for imperfection extended to his possessions and his staff. A broken piece of furniture would be discarded rather than repaired. He refused to hire one maid because she had a lisp and another who had a limp. The psychologist he had seen as a child diagnosed this obsessive behavior of having everything fit in with his standards of perfection as atelophobia. This disease would now change his life and the lives of the children he fathered.

As he entered his house, a tall, well-groomed butler approached to take his coat. "Sorry about your loss, sir," he stated.

"Thank you, Edward." Getting directly to the point, as he always did, he said, "My son..." He stopped for a moment to compose his words. "Robert Ludlow Jr. will be coming home Tuesday. Please have the staff ready the nursery. And..." he said with just a hint of a tremor in his voice, "please ask the nurse if she can stay on in a more permanent position. I will need someone to care for the child." He immediately went upstairs to his office. If he was sad about the loss of his wife, it was not apparent.

He arose early Monday morning for his meeting with the director of the Bayside Children's Home, an orphanage located in a rural area of Connecticut. The director, Orin Barrow, was well connected. Robert Sr. was given his name through a state senator who also made the introduction. The orphanage was on the outskirts of Tamarine, a town west of Danbury. Driving to the orphanage was like being transported back in time. Tall trees lined the long driveway from the two-lane road to the manor of an old estate. Legend had it that the stones that made up the granite facade were carried by boat from England in the late nineteenth century. The facility itself was located at the site of an old estate that locals still talked about. The prior owner disappeared one night. He was later found in a shallow makeshift grave several towns away. Asphyxiation due to strangulation, the medical examiner's report stated. He died intestate. The property was quickly sold at auction to a firm that belonged to the present owner, Orin Barrow. Director Barrow, as he was called, owned several similar orphanages. All purchased after similar tragedies. Orphanage regulations were all but nonexistent at the time, and what transpired behind the closed doors of the facility was not known. He was a master marketer and both solicited and obtained significant contributions from many well-respected philanthropists. This resulted in his orphanages gaining national acclaim even though there were rumors of his profiting in the private placement of babies.

The governor was driven to the Bayside Children's Home in his 1953 Cadillac Fleetwood limousine. He loved cars and was very particular regarding those he purchased. He was particularly enamored by the Series 75 model styling, which introduced the chrome eyebrow-like headlamp covers. He entered through the twelve-foot-high darkly stained oak doors. He was greeted by an attractive female staff member who opened the door knowingly as he approached.

"Welcome to the Bayside Children's Home, Mr. Ludlow. Mr. Barrow asked that I take you to his office."

The entrance foyer was large with a wide staircase on the right, leading up from the main floor. Sounds echoed from the white marble floors and twenty-foot-high ceilings. The walls were adorned with paintings from several masters. *Interesting decor for an orphanage,* the governor thought. The governor was escorted to an office on the main floor positioned across the from the oak doors. He passed through another darkly stained oak door, this one a nine-foot-high door that led into an antechamber just outside the director's office.

"Mr. Ludlow, please have a seat. The director will be with you in a moment." The secretary motioned to an elegant couch. "Can I get you anything?"

"No, thank you," the governor replied.

A second nine-foot-high oak door opened prior to his answering. A stout man in his forties with a receding hairline and slicked-back hair entered. "Mr. Ludlow, I am Orin Barrow. It was good speaking with you yesterday." They shook hands as Barrow motioned him into the office and asked him to sit in an overstuffed chesterfield armchair facing the windows. Barrow sat behind a large maple desk with relics of his travels prominently displayed. The back wall of the office had expansive windows overlooking the manicured gardens.

"I must say," Barrow continued, "I was intrigued by the proposal you mentioned on the phone. How would you propose proceeding?"

"Mr. Barrow, what I say to you must be kept in strict confidence. I will request that you personally sign a contract agreeing to these terms. Shall I continue?" the governor asked before continuing.

"Yes, please proceed," Barrow replied.

"There were two children just born who I want to be admitted to the Bayside Children's Home. A primary trust will be set up for their care and future educational needs. I would like you to be the trustee until a child is adopted. Then the adoptive parents would become the trustee. Should either of the children die, the remainder will go to the surviving child." There was no inflection in the governor's voice as he said the word *die.* He then continued, "When the children reach twenty-five, the balance of the monies in their trust will be deposited in bank accounts in their names and under their control. For your efforts as trustee, you will receive a salary each month from the primary trust." The governor looked over at Barrow for any facial expression. There was none, even though this arrangement was certainly unethical and possibly illegal. "And one additional requirement." The governor waited for Barrow's response.

"And what is that?" Barrow asked as if on cue.

"No entity shall know of my involvement in this agreement. Records of this agreement, as well as that of the babies, must be kept secret. Is this something you can agree to?" Ludlow concluded.

Without hesitation Barrow stated, "Absolutely!" And with that the deal was made.

4

ORPHANAGE

Tuesday, September 20, 1955

The trust document was delivered to Barrow's office the next day. He read it immediately and made a few changes to the document, further assuring his control of the assets. Ludlow Sr. did not have a problem with that, although he probably should have. If he was thinking clearly, and not under the pressure to make this deal quickly, he would have argued for at least a second trustee. But he didn't. The director also requested a provision that if the adoptive parents declined the trust, then the monies would revert to the primary trust. These changes essentially allowed an unscrupulous man like the director to use the monies for his own interests. The changes were agreed upon and signed.

The first baby was delivered to the orphanage on Friday morning. A hospital ambulance drove up to the orphanage to be greeted by a nurse and attendant. It was a windy day, as fall was underway. The clouds obscured the sunlight. One of the first leaves to fall landed in the bassinet holding the baby, who grasped the dying leaf with his right hand. It likely contributed to his being named Dexter by the orphanage.

The baby was taken to the nursery, where eight other babies were lined up in a perfectly ordered row. The room was small and without windows, which made the smell of urine and feces even more unpleasant. The nursery was also located in a different wing and on a higher floor than the rooms for the older children. The infants were fed on schedule and slept on schedule. No deviation was allowed. The newborn infants had few visitors. The nurses had time during the day only to hold the babies during feeding time. No kissing, no hugging, and limited patting to expel the swallowed air. Medical journals had been replete with articles on the psychological scars that the lack of human contact and love, especially during the first five years of life, had on children. Besides these psychological scars, children had died as a result of failure to thrive, their immune systems turned off with the loss of love during this formative period. There were several experimental studies in litters of puppies and kittens that showed deficiency in love resulted in stunting of growth and development. This phenomenon was so well known that it was referred to as the "runt syndrome."

A nurse's aide brought baby Dexter to a changing table in the nursery located next to a bassinet that had been recently vacated. That baby had graduated to a crib in the room down the hall. She was alone in the nursery. She unwrapped the blanket that was swaddling the infant and rolled up the long undershirt. As she took down the cloth diaper, she let out a guttural gasp. As if shocked by electricity, she fell suddenly backward, only being stopped by the bassinet, which was prevented from falling over by its crashing into the wall behind it.

"Oh my dear God!" she cried out, her face pale and her hands shaking.

She was horrified by what she saw. She needed to sit to regain her composure. She pulled the only stool in the room over to the table. She had been a nurse's aide for thirty years and had never seen this before. *Was it a boy or girl?* she thought as she regained her composure. Others came running in, thinking she been injured—or worse.

Where the term first came from was not known. However, they started to refer to baby Dexter as the devil's child. Most of the staff were too afraid to take care of him. Only one German nurse—in fact, the only registered nurse who worked in the orphanage, Nurse Brunswick—was not repulsed by the infant's malady. She had a family member who had a similar condition. The infant was soon known as Dexter Brunswick. When Nurse Brunswick was off, Dexter often went for a day or more with a soiled diaper. He would continually cry. No one would come. When Nurse Brunswick would return, she would find his skin breaking down and castigate the nurse's aide who was supposed to take care of him. But most of the nurse's aides were too superstitious. They felt an evil aura surrounding Dexter. They wanted to live. She made the director aware. One would have thought that Orin Barrow, the trustee of a large sum of money for the benefit of this child, would have been more concerned. He wasn't. He spoke with the aides. He felt he had to. But nothing changed.

A nurse from the hospital delivered the second baby to the orphanage early in the morning several weeks later. This baby was so traumatized by his birth he required weeks of intensive care just to survive. They needed to wait until the baby was stable enough to be transferred. This nurse insisted on being the nurse to accompany the baby to the orphanage. She was in the delivery room when he was born and had just spent every day and night caring for as well as kissing and hugging this baby since he was born. She had named this baby Kevin after her recently deceased father, whom she had loved so much. She could not tolerate calling the baby "Baby Boy Three," as stated on his birth certificate. The bond now was unbreakable. She spent the morning observing the operation of the orphanage. She saw a baby left in an unchanged diaper for hours. Others left crying without being consoled by the staff. Her heart was breaking. She could not bear the thought of leaving the child she now considered *her* baby in this environment. She knew what she had to do. She walked to the office to speak with the director.

The nurse entered the director's office, not knowing what the response would be but determined to protect this child. She had no idea that her plan would fit perfectly with the director's grand scheme.

"How can I help you?" the secretary asked.

"I would like to see the director," she replied.

"Do you have an appointment?" the secretary asked, knowing full well that she didn't.

"I am a nurse from Bayside Hospital. I just brought a baby to your orphanage," she stated, ignoring the question that was just asked. "I would like to adopt this baby," she stated.

"You will need to fill out these papers first," the secretary said, handing her a large folder of papers. She was also given orders from the director to alert him to anyone contacting the orphanage wanting to adopt a child from Bayside Hospital. She quietly pushed the intercom microphone button so the director could hear the conversation.

"I understand the need for protocol," she responded. "I have just spent some time in your nursery. The staff is obviously busy with so many infants in need," she stated, trying to be diplomatic. "I have a special bond with this infant and would like to assure his safety." The implication was clear, although not stated, that she, a nurse from Bayside Hospital, felt that the care was less than acceptable.

With that a light lit up on the secretary's phone. She answered. "Yes, sir. Yes, sir," she replied. She turned back to the nurse. "The director's morning meeting was just canceled. Let me see if he can see you." With that she stood up, walked to the director's office, and entered. She closed the door behind her.

The nurse was surprised at what had just happened but took it in stride. *Whatever gets the desired result,* she thought. The door then opened, and the secretary beckoned her into the director's office.

"Good day, nurse. How may I help you?" the director asked.

The nurse introduced herself and poured her soul out. "I have taken care of this baby since he was born. I am in love with this baby.

Please let me know how to make this adoption happen," she stated with tears rolling down her cheeks.

The director was pleased with her response. He knew this baby was one of the two Ludlow babies. He also knew that if he had her sign a waiver, the trust monies would remain under his control. He responded, "I can see you are so in love with this baby. This child would be so lucky to have you as his adoptive mother. There are rules, however, we must comply with. You will have to complete the forms."

The nurse quickly responded, "Of course."

He then asked, "Are you financially secure enough to take care of this child?"

Although she was not sure what he was really asking, she did not want to be adversarial. "Yes, of course."

"Good," he continued. "We have a lot of less-fortunate children here who don't find supportive families like yours. We have benefactors who donate large sums of money to help us care for these children." He then paused to see her reaction and compose his next sentence. "We often have funds for children who are adopted to help their families but encourage the adoptive families who are financially secure, like yours, to sign a waiver so that these funds can go to others who are less fortunate."

"Of course, of course," she blurted out, thinking only of the baby she loved so much.

After she signed the waiver, the director made sure the adoption went through.

5

METAMORPHOSIS

With a loving family, surgery would have been performed around one year of age. But Dexter Brunswick did not have a loving family. Delivered to an orphanage a few days after birth, he was at the mercy of others for cleaning and feeding. Only Nurse Brunswick was his caretaker. The religious nurse's aides remained fearful. They were practitioners of a less common form of voodoo. In their religion, the body and soul were inextricably linked. They were convinced that the deformities in his genitalia were the real-world manifestations of an evil soul. They felt this. They believed this. They feared this.

The first two years of life for an orphan are often the prime years for adoption. Prospective parents looking for a child want an infant naive to the world. Many children in the orphanage were adopted or placed in foster care during these first two years of life. But not Dexter. On several occasions, Dexter was interviewed by a prospective family. Each time, Dexter would do something that quickly ended the interview. One time, at the age of two, he entered the interview room and started crying. He didn't stop until the family left the room, covering their ears. Two years later, when he was four, he picked up a toy block, which was placed on the floor for him to play with during the interview. He hurled it at the prospective foster mother, leaving a welt on her forehead and no chance of a placement.

Orin Barrow did not intervene when he overheard the other orphans taunting Dexter. Some thought he even encouraged it. There was no hiding his abnormal genitalia during the daily group shower. He was made to shower with the group and resented it. He refused, and he was punished. Spanking when he was young and paddling as he got older.

Dexter kept to himself as a young child. Possibly he knew, even as an infant, that the world had abandoned him. The older orphans tormented him. That all changed on his sixth birthday. The only kindness the orphanage seemed to bestow on the orphans was recognition of their birthday with a cupcake. Ceremoniously, the staff would carry it out at lunch, and all would sing "Happy Birthday." Something was amiss with Dexter that September day. He ran from the dining hall as the staff and single cupcake approached. He hated them. He did not know how to express these feelings. They just grew inside him.

That afternoon an eight-year-old orphan boy approached him in the field next to the orphanage where boys were playing ball. It was a cloudy day with rain expected. A chill was in the air. Most of the high-school-aged boys in the orphanage were required to study during this time and were inside. Only the younger boys were on the field. This eight-year-old boy walked over to Dexter, who was standing by himself next to the equipment supply bag that had been brought out for the game. A few of the eight-year-old's friends were with him. He must have felt empowered.

"Hey, devil's child!" he yelled out as he encroached on Dexter's personal space.

The eight-year-old must have heard a nurse's aide call him that. Dexter tried pushing him away, but the eight-year-old's arm was already in motion and hit Dexter squarely in the face, knocking him to the ground. Something snapped in Dexter at that very moment. The eight-year-old turned to his friends laughing, not seeing what Dexter was planning. Dexter got up with a bat in his hand. He walked calmly over to the eight-year-old and hit him in the chest as the eight-year-old turned. This knocked the wind out of the eight-year-old and sent him falling to the ground. It didn't stop at that. Dexter was merciless in pummeling the eight-year-old into an unconscious state with the now bloodied bat as the other children watched. Some cried; all were in disbelief. A staff member from the orphanage ran to break up the assault. The eight-year-old was taken to the hospital. The eight-year-old suffered a concussion with "bleeding on the brain," one doctor said. He was never the same afterward. Dexter calmly walked back to the orphanage. There was no evidence of emotion of any kind. No child ever picked on Dexter again.

Orin Barrow was seemingly uninvolved during Dexter's first six formative years. Nurse Brunswick on several occasions pleaded with him to get this young boy help. The director kept insisting that there were no funds available. What would they have said to him if they knew of the trust? The assault in the field was the defining event. The director would likely have looked the other way, but the police and state authorities insisted on an evaluation of Dexter. It was probably too late. Was it nature or nurture? Both were likely formative for Dexter Brunswick.

A social worker was mandated by the Department of Child Welfare to evaluate and treat Dexter. She was required to submit daily and weekly reports to the department. He would sit in the room with the social worker, just looking at her with inward-slanting eyebrows that were squeezed together and a furrowed brow. His lowered head, pursed lips, and the forward thrust of his jaw were downright frightening. The social worker assigned to him felt unsafe remaining in the same room with him. The orphanage assigned an aide to accompany her during these sessions. The director reluctantly used some of the trust's funds to cover the cost of the aide and the psychological tests that were ordered.

Even after months of therapy, there were no results. Dexter showed no remorse for his attack on the eight-year-old. In fact, he felt entitled. He continually refused to cooperate. However, the reports sent back by the social worker were enough to calm the state authorities, which took pressure off the orphanage and the director. Dexter's IQ score was over 140, which placed him in the genius category. Possibly it was the continual taunting by the other orphans or almost routine emotional and corporal punishment by the staff that changed Dexter. Or maybe it was something he inherited. This young boy was deeply troubled with an angry fire burning within.

The attack of the eight-year-old in the field changed Orin Barrow's involvement. The director became directly involved in discipline of the boys in the orphanage. Particularly that of Dexter. State regulations no longer permitted corporal punishment from being used in orphanages. That didn't stop the director from using other punishments.

Dexter Brunswick had only one friend in the orphanage. That one boy was Avery.

Avery's mother was unmarried when he was born. She met this boy at a party thrown by one of her friends whose parents just happened to be away for the weekend. She had never had a screwdriver or drunk any alcoholic beverage before. That night she had five. She also had her first sexual encounter that night. She knew she was pregnant when she missed two periods. She was always regular. She was also having tenderness in her breasts. She never told the father she was pregnant. Or anyone. She was a bit overweight and always wore loose-fitting tops. She was only seventeen when Avery was born in the basement of his mother's house. She bundled Avery up and walked. She did not have the energy to run the two blocks to the nearby hospital. She had been planning this for several months. What she didn't plan was the amount of bleeding she was experiencing. Blood continually soaked through her pants even though she had taken a towel and stuffed it in her pants before she left the house. She entered the waiting area of the emergency department, looking carefully to make sure no one she knew was there. Her blood-soaked clothes left a trail.

She felt so weak but knew she couldn't stop. She left her crying baby on a seat next to an elderly gray-haired woman. Avery's mother's lifeless body was found in the hospital parking lot just outside the emergency room an hour later.

Avery was born with a wide-open cleft lip and palate. When he was given formula as an infant, most would spill out before he could swallow any. Swallowing was often interrupted by gagging and sneezing as formula, unfettered, entered the nasal cavity. Medical care was difficult to obtain for the orphan. Usually these defects would be corrected by six months to one year of age. Avery's first surgery was not until he was almost four years old. It was likely done by an inexperienced surgeon, given the pronounced scar he was left with. Avery understood the stigma of being different, which created the bond between Dexter and him.

Avery shared Dexter's hatred of the orphanage and especially the other orphans and staff. He and Dexter would occasionally join forces to get even. One time they added bleach to several of the shampoo bottles and placed them strategically in the shower room. Many orphans' hair turned blond. Several of the orphans also lost their vision, as the bleach burned their corneas. Avery and Dexter took showers at the same time, sharing a tainted shampoo bottle, making sure to close their eyes tightly, so as not to arouse suspicion. It worked. No one ever found out who had tainted the shampoo. The move to lace several, but not all, the bottles was genius, since it also served to incite fear in the other orphans.

The director became increasingly less involved in the day-to-day running of the orphanage. He had siphoned off much of the trust money by the time Dexter was twelve. He was also under continued investigation by the state child welfare department for his management of this and several other orphanages he owned and ran. These investigations, together with a fraud investigation by the tax department for appropriating funds from his orphanages, ultimately forced him to sell off all his orphanages before Dexter turned eighteen.

Eighteen years of age marks a special time in the lives of orphans. At eighteen, they age out. They can no longer stay in the orphanage and will move to a group home if they have no alternative plans. Statistics showed that most orphans who age out have bleak futures. Many do not graduate from high school and remain on public assistance for the rest of their lives. This was not going to be true for Dexter. He excelled in classes, even though he rarely attended. His standardized college entrance test scores were so high that he was given a scholarship for full tuition and room and board at Brown University. Avery was not as fortunate. He was moved to a group home and given a job in a food warehouse.

It was the week prior to midterms in his senior year at Brown. Dexter Brunswick was in the habit of checking his mailbox in the apartment building since applying to medical schools. He was waiting for their responses. Just a few days ago he received an acceptance to one of his top choices, the University of Virginia School of Medicine. He applied for financial aid and again received a full ride with tuition and room and board. He was also guaranteed a job on campus for spending money. He was waiting for others to reply, possibly with additional money not tied to his working, before making his decision.

Among the junk mail that he received was a business envelope addressed to him with the return address of the Bayside Children's Home. He clenched his fists as his bite tightened. His sweaty palms stained the envelope. Curious as it was to receive a letter from the orphanage, he was ready to throw it in the trash, but then he wondered how they knew where to find him. Orin Barrow had left his position at the orphanage over three years prior. He had been found guilty of a misdemeanor and ordered to pay restitution of $30,000, which he gladly did since that was only a fraction of what he had stolen. He had a great lawyer. Dexter had read the article about this and thought the punishment should be greater. Much greater. He decided to open the letter. The letter, postmarked December 3, 1977, was from the new director, Alan Presley, who was hired by the orphanage's board of trustees partly because of his background in theology. He had earned his doctorate in Divinity and had been a pastor for over ten years. They hoped his background would overshadow the bad reputation that the orphanage had after the revelation of Orin Barrow's scandalous actions.

It read:

> *Dear Dexter Brunswick,*
>
> *I first would like to congratulate you on your achievements. We have followed your success and have learned that you were recently admitted to medical school and will be graduating from college with high honors. We at the orphanage are so proud that we were part of your life achievements.*
>
> *We have found some items that your biological father left for you and thought you might be able to come by to pick them up. When you plan to come by, please call so I can make sure that I am here to give them to you personally.*
>
> *Sincerely,*
> *Alan Presley, DD*
> *Director, Bayside Children's Home*

Dexter was disgusted by the first part of the letter. "Bastards!" he exclaimed. "These are the same people who made my life a living hell for eighteen years, and they're now taking credit for my 'achievements.'" He was, however, intrigued by the second part of the letter. "Items from my biological father?" he stated as if the director were in the room with him. "They knew who my father was?" he queried. With that, he picked up the phone and arranged to meet with the new director in two days.

He arrived at the nearest town by bus. Having no money, he needed to hitchhike to the Bayside Children's Home. The trip that would usually take two and a half hours by car took him six hours. Very different from the way the governor had arrived twenty-two years ago.

An attractive brunette about Dexter's age brought him in to see the new director, Alan Presley, in his first-floor office. She had known about Dexter's achievements.

"You are quite a celebrity around here!" she exclaimed, flicking her long dark-brown hair.

Dexter had no interest in her. How could he? A relationship could not go anywhere. "Is the director here?" he asked, curtly looking around the empty room. The director's office was quite different than when he was last there. In place of the elegant stuffed couches were simple wooden office chairs. Commercial lithographs had replaced the paintings, probably sold off to pay for operating expenses after Orin Barrow sold most of the orphanage's assets to pay his debts.

"Yes, he will be right back. Please have a seat. He will be right with you," she replied.

The director entered the room. Dexter Brunswick remained seated.

"Thank you for coming. Good to meet you!" the director exclaimed with an outstretched hand.

Dexter did not extend his hand in response. "You have items that are mine?" he asked bluntly.

The director stepped back and took his seat across the desk from Dexter. His demeanor changed from friendly to serious. Dexter used this time to look around the room. He had been in the room on only two occasions: the first after the incident with the eight-year-old and the second on the day he left the orphanage for good. He didn't remember the director's office being as small as it was or the beautiful gardens and tall trees outside the director's office windows. He also didn't remember seeing another door in the office with a bolt lock and plaque that read File Room prominently positioned on the door. *Odd,* he thought, *to have a file room inside another office.*

"Yes," the director began. "As you might know, the orphanage was sold after Orin Barrow's departure."

Dexter acknowledged with a nod of his head, and the director continued, "Because of questions regarding the financial integrity of the orphanage, the new owners commissioned a forensic accounting firm to investigate. They found that Mr. Barrow had been siphoning money to accounts that he solely controlled—"

Dexter Brunswick interrupted. "And why are you telling me this?"

The director continued a softer and more direct approach to assuage the aggressive attitude of Dexter Brunswick. "One of the accounts that he pilfered was a trust set up by your biological father for his two sons, born September 16, 1955."

Dexter felt his eyelids opening widely and his jaw dropping. "You mean to tell me I have a brother…a twin brother?" he asked incredulously with less concern for the money Orin Barrow had stolen.

"Well, according to this trust document…which I have made a copy of for you…" he said, taking a document from a full manila file folder. A now standing Dexter Brunswick immediately snatched the document from his hands. The director grew concerned about Dexter Brunswick's mental stability.

"Who is my father? And who and where is my brother?" Dexter stated emphatically. "And where is the trust money?"

"Please calm down," the director pleaded, motioning with his arms for Dexter to be seated. "Some answers we know and others we do not."

Dexter sat back in the chair as the director continued, "The trust was set up with Orin Barrow as the sole trustee. Only he knows the name of your father." This was a lie, but the director was truly concerned that Dexter Brunswick might seek out and harass a benefactor of the orphanage. "As for your brother, we do not know." Another lie.

Dexter's face tightened with his eyes wide and fixated on the director. The director continued with a softer voice. "We have no record of another boy being admitted to the orphanage with your birth date. He might have been privately adopted."

"Where is Orin Barrow now?" Dexter demanded, knowing that only Barrow knew the answers to the questions.

"We don't know. And quite frankly, even if we did, we would not be able to tell you," he stated sincerely.

"Is there anything else you have for me?" Dexter inquired, knowing that what he had just learned was all the director knew.

"Unfortunately not," the director replied.

Dexter got up from his chair with the trust document in hand and left without any further conversation. He now had a focus for his hatred. His mind was set on what he had to do.

6

CHARACTER

Bob Ludlow Jr. grew up in a privileged world. A cadre of servants cared for him. His father was not often around, and he spent little time with his son when he was there. He attended the prestigious boarding school Choate and then Yale University. He, like his estranged brother, were gifted with extraordinary intelligence. The similarities, however, stopped there. Bob Ludlow Jr. would often be found at the soup kitchen helping on holidays. On more than one occasion he found an injured animal either in or on the side of the road, and he'd stop his car to pick up the animal and nurse it back to health as he searched for the owner.

He was a quiet, self-deprecating person who earned the respect of his many friends for his compassion. He was also a talented cross-country runner during his boarding school days. These races were often run through the countryside in all weather conditions.

The team remembered one race at the end of the season when competition was intense. Only one runner could be chosen to represent the school at the state championships. Three of the team's twelve runners were in contention, and the final race of the season was approaching. Bob was one of the three. It was raining lightly the day of the race. During the last half of the three-mile race, he was second with the lead runner fifty feet in front of him. The third-position runner was far behind him. The lead runner was a senior, with Bob being only a sophomore. They were not close friends, but Bob respected him as a more experienced teammate. He knew he would have to make his push. So too did the lead runner. There was a rocky downhill portion not more than three hundred yards from the finish line as the trail bent to the right. There was a sharp drop on the left into a ravine. This area was not visible from behind or from the finish line. The lead runner was poised to win. As the lead runner rounded the turn to the right, he must have slipped on a wet stone. His feet went out from under him. Bob saw him falling and then sliding to the left, down into the ravine. He saw the lead runner hit his head on a rock as his body rolled down the hill like a rag doll. Bob slowed up as he approached the point of the accident and saw that the runner was not moving. He could have finished the race and won and then returned for the injured runner. The finish line was only fifty yards ahead. But that was not Bob. Without giving it a second thought, he slid down the hill toward the ravine and shouted to the other runners to get help as they passed him by on to the finish line.

7

EPIPHANY

Years had passed since Dexter's meeting with Alan Presley. Dexter had graduated Yale Medical School summa cum laude. He had given up the full ride offered by the University of Virginia School of Medicine when the Yale offer came in. The Yale offer did not include room and board; however, he was offered a paid position working in the genetics lab, which clinched the deal. Like all his other schooling, he found most of it boring. He had a photographic memory and would ace tests just by reading the textbooks and written transcriptions by his classmates. Each medical student was assigned several lectures to transcribe during the year. That meant you had to attend the lecture, which Brunswick would not do. Brunswick also had a semantic memory. He could memorize a deck of randomly arranged cards in under twenty seconds. He was unbeatable at many card games. He leveraged his winnings in cards to entice his classmates to transcribe the lectures he was assigned.

It is common for physicians to migrate toward fields they have a personal connection to. This was true for Brunswick. Genetics and embryology intrigued him. He would read all he could on these subjects. He had met with the professors in these courses, hoping to get answers to questions he had to extend his knowledge but found them too ignorant. He developed his own theories. By his second year in medical school he had submitted a patent for a novel way to identify areas on the Y chromosome that people thought were related to sperm production.

He also continued his search for his past. He wanted to confront the father who had abandoned him and meet a brother who shared his plight. His primary focus was on finding Orin Barrow, the director of the orphanage who made his life a living hell in the orphanage and who absconded with monies meant for him. He wanted revenge for the ravages he endured under his watch and now for the theft of money due him. But he also needed him. Orin Barrow was the only one who knew the identity of his biological father and brother. Orin Barrow was not an easy man to find. Brunswick had tried the usual ways to locate the man through telephone directories and public records. Barrow was found guilty of a misdemeanor. He paid restitution and dissolved his businesses. He disappeared, although it was rumored he still had significant funds stashed away.

Dexter had read the trust document many times, trying to get additional clues. Names of the children were not listed. Only the trustee's name, Orin Barrow, appeared. The trust only listed Baby A and Baby B, who were delivered to the orphanage. He had tried the law firm that was listed on the document, but they had long since closed their doors. He even tried the bank that was listed as the holder of the trust funds and was told that the remaining funds had been seized by the state once the fraud was uncovered. They stated they did not know who the beneficiaries were. Brunswick's obsession with finding Orin Barrow grew as the years went by. He had completed his fellowship, also at Yale, and started a private practice specializing in male fertility in Stamford, Connecticut.

It was Friday, September 16, 1988. Brunswick was thirty-three that day. He never celebrated his birthday after the orphanage experience. That day there was to be a guest lecturer at the hospital grand rounds who was going to talk about one of the few subjects that fascinated him—the translocations of genes from one chromosome to another. He thought that was what he would do on his birthday. He was reading the newspaper and came across a human-interest article about the son of a philanthropist, Robert Ludlow Jr., whose birthday was that day also. Ludlow was celebrating by gifting new playground equipment to an orphanage his family had supported financially for over three decades. Brunswick would not have continued reading that story except that it stated that the orphanage was the Bayside Children's Home. *Could it be?* he thought. Could this be his brother? Same birth date, and the family had been supporting the orphanage from the time he was there.

He was on his way to the lecture when he stopped in his tracks and cried out loud, "Damn, I am going to find out. I am going to find out today!" The reaction was like the abrupt personality change he experienced at six years of age. No one was around to hear him. He really didn't care if there was. He knew where he needed to go. This time he had a car.

The drive to the Bayside Children's Home took under two hours. The sun was setting by the time he was near the orphanage. He preferred it that way. He knew most of the administrative staff would have already left for the day. A single-lane road led up to the orphanage. It was a half mile up this road from the main highway. Brunswick decided to park at a diner off the main highway and walk to the orphanage. He parked in an area that was hidden from both the road and occupants of the diner. He took a small flashlight and screwdriver from the glove compartment and put them in the pocket of his coat. He decided to eat at the diner first. He figured it would take him twenty or thirty minutes to walk to the orphanage. He wanted it to be dark. He had his gloves on as he walked. The trees arching over the single-lane road blocked the moonlight. The baseball field was on his right, with the main building to the left. The field was brighter, lit up by the full moon. Brunswick kept out of the light as he made his way to the back of the house. It was dark outside the large windows behind the director's desk. The trees obscured the moonlight. The only sound was the light evening wind wafting through the trees. He took out his flashlight to help him find his way. He was headed to the file room door inside the office. He found one of the large windows slightly ajar. He pushed it open and climbed in. The office windows faced a small grassy area with tall trees. The office had little moonlight entering through the windows. He took out his flashlight. He made his way to the file room door. "Not much for security. Never was," he muttered. The only security the door had was a cheap padlock. He tore the bracket from the door easily with the screwdriver. He opened the file room door.

He found the light switch and closed the door before turning the light on. It was a relatively small room for a file room. It was about eight feet deep and six feet wide. It had two rows of file cabinets with old office equipment lying on top of the cabinets. The file drawers were labeled in five-year increments starting 1945–1949. Brunswick opened the 1955–1959 file cabinet. It was packed with files overflowing with documents. Each folder had a family name followed by a date. He needed to take a few files out to be able to read the folder names on the rest. He looked for a file dated September 16, 1955. The date of his birth.

He found a folder marked "Ludlow—September 16, 1955." *Interesting,* he thought. He took it out and opened it, not knowing that what he was about to find would set a new direction for his life. Inside was a copy of the trust document he already had. However, this copy had an addendum dated April 3, 1985. It was shortly after that date that Orin Barrow was arrested for stealing funds from the orphanages' accounts. It amended the original trust by adding a Donald Gifford as trustee. *Who was Donald Gifford?* he thought. There were also two birth certificates. They were both short birth certificates. They listed only the date of birth and the surname Ludlow. "So the new director lied to me. Not much different from the old one," Brunswick muttered. There were no given names other than Baby Boy Two and Baby Boy Three. *What?* he thought. *There are three boys? Who and where is Baby Boy One?*

The birth certificate for Baby Two had a time of birth; however, that for Baby Three did not. *Curious,* he thought. There was nothing else in the manila folder. He placed all files back in the drawer as he found them. He didn't need to take anything with him. He had already committed what he had read to memory. *The hospital,* he thought. *That would be the best place to start.* But only the city, Stamford, Connecticut, was noted on the birth certificate. *Even if the hospital's name was known,* he thought, *it might not even be still in existence, given the financial trouble so many hospitals are in.*

He was turning to leave when his eye caught a file cabinet with a green label, which was a stark contrast to most of the others that were white with black typed lettering. He walked over to read the label: "Employee Files." He opened the cabinet. He looked for only one file, the file for the person he held responsible for making his life a living hell at the orphanage. Orin Barrow. In the back of the cabinet there was a section marked "Prior Employees." In that section, he found a folder labeled "Orin Barrow." He opened it and found an address: 21 East Chester Drive, Lake Shore. He made sure that all files were placed back the way he found them. He was on his way.

It was a short drive to Lake Shore from the orphanage and approaching midnight as Brunswick entered the town of Lake Shore. The town was named for its location on the banks of one of the largest manmade lakes in Connecticut for hydroelectric power generation in 1926. It was a small rural town with a single main road that ran through town. Deer were plentiful, which brought many hunters to the area during the season. There were several tree stands built by hunters and placed in the tall trees lining the edges of the corn and clover fields that surrounded the town. Orin Barrow's house was two miles out of town off a small country road. His property was fifty-five acres with a sprawling six-thousand-square-foot ranch house centered on the property. There were barns for horses. The winding road leading up to the house was at least a mile from the small country road.

Barrow had married when he was young but divorced within five years. Since moving into this immense space, he had lived alone. He had a nurse with him during the day to help with his diabetic control, which had become particularly difficult over the last several years. He had been hospitalized several times, which precipitated his hiring the nurse. He never made much from the orphanage business, but he was a master of the deal and would find innovative—often dishonest—ways to fill his coffers. Like his pilfering of the Ludlow trust. He had others helping him during the day but preferred his seclusion at night.

The lights were off in the house when Brunswick arrived. He had parked the car off to the side of the small winding road halfway to the main house. The evening was not that cool, yet he had his gloves on as he approached the house. He did not want to be disturbed when he was questioning the director. He looked for the power and telephone lines and saw that they led directly to the garage. He walked around to the back of the garage and used his screwdriver to pry open the door in the back of the garage. He entered and used his flashlight to locate the power box and then flipped the main breaker. Next to it was a small telephone box. He opened it and disconnected the main telephone line. There was a second door in the garage that led into the main house. He again entered by prying the door latch away from the doorjamb. He was in the house.

He made his way across a small room that had a television set and couch and led into the kitchen. He found a used insulin syringe on the kitchen counter. He picked it up with his gloved hand. He opened the refrigerator and took the bottle of insulin that he was sure would be there. He filled the syringe with the insulin and put both in his pocket. He could hear snoring coming from a room down the hall from the kitchen. It was dark, and all he could see was the area lit up by his flashlight.

Orin Barrow was awakened by a gloved hand covering his mouth and the needle of the syringe piercing a large vessel in his neck. He dared not move.

Brunswick asked calmly. “Who was Dexter Brunswick’s father, and where can he be found?”

Without hesitation, he stated, "Robert Ludlow Sr. They call him the governor. The Ludlow estate in Erie County."

"Who is Donald Gifford, and where is the second child who was brought to the orphanage?" Brunswick then demanded.

"Donald Gifford is the governor's estranged brother," Barrow said with a weakening voice.

"And who adopted that second child?" Brunswick continued.

"I don't remember. But if you let me make a call to the orphanage, then I can find out," the director said, slurring his words.

"No need to. I'll find out," Brunswick said as he emptied the remaining insulin into the director's neck. He didn't realize how vital this information would have been if he had not been so impatient. He waited fifteen minutes as the director became unconscious. In another fifteen minutes, he was pulseless.

Brunswick walked to the kitchen, placed the insulin back in the refrigerator, and set the syringe on the counter. He exited through the garage and closed the door to the house, hooked the telephone line back up, and flipped on the main circuit breaker. He closed the door in the back of the garage. He had a smile on his face as he walked calmly back to his car.

Orin Barrow's nurse found him dead when she arrived in the morning. She called an ambulance. The police followed shortly behind. He was pronounced dead at the house, and it became a medical examiner's case and police investigation.

A new detective, Kevin O'Brien, was assigned to the case with a Detective Tollins. Tollins was a few years older than Detective O'Brien and had been a detective for two years already. The medical examiner decided the cause of death was an insulin overdose. The syringe had only the victim's fingerprints on it. The older detective, who was responsible for making the final decision on the case, thought it was a simple suicide of an elderly man in failing health who was stressed out by multiple legal entanglements. The younger Detective O'Brien was not convinced.

"Why did both the door to the house and the garage appear to have evidence of forcible entry?" he questioned his mentor.

"Could have been done years prior when he locked himself out of the house. And besides, what would be the motive? There was no family fighting, and his employees needed the income. Besides, his will left his estate to the Bayside orphanage."

It all sounded plausible to Detective O'Brien. But he was still not convinced.

8

ANCESTRY

Kevin O'Brien was a sickly baby and almost died at birth. His mother died giving birth. His adoptive mother, Caitlin, was a nurse in the delivery room when he was born. She immediately fell in love with this infant in need of love and caring that only a family could provide. She also had the requisite skills.

Catlin was almost forty when she met her adoptive son. He was brought home from the orphanage to this good Irish family. They had tried many years to have children of their own but were not blessed in that way. Instead they were given the great gift of caring for a child in need.

Kevin found out he was adopted at the age of fourteen. He had been looking in his father's desk drawer for a pencil to do his math homework and found a folder lying on top of the pencils. When he lifted the folder, it hit the side of the desk and landed on the floor. A frayed piece of paper fell out. He picked up the paper and opened the folder to put it back in. It was the embossed seal that got his attention. On top, it read "Certificate of Birth." Below, it listed only the name, Baby Three Ludlow, and date of birth, September 16, 1955. In the folder, there was another birth certificate. This appeared to be the long-form birth certificate and listed both the child, Kevin, and his parents, Cathleen and David O'Brien. The hospital of birth was

Bayside Hospital. He placed all back in the folder and set the folder back in his father's desk.

It was at dinner that evening, which the family always had together, that he innocently asked his father, "Hey, Dad, I was looking for a pen in your desk and found a folder with my birth certificate and another birth certificate with Baby Three on it. I was wondering what that was."

His father stopped eating and looked over at his wife. They were motionless as they stared incredulously at each other. They knew this moment would occur but were not prepared for it. As if ever a family can be. They had made the decision recently to tell their son about the adoption but just didn't know how or when. He had taken the birth certificates from the safe and placed them in his desk with the intent of discussing them with their son, never thinking that Kevin would find the folder with both certificates inside. The opportunity was now.

He turned to his son. "Kevin, you know we love you very much. We are so proud of you and could not have asked for a better child. But there is something we have not told you. Something we really did not know how to tell you. However, I see that now is the time to let you know."

"What is it, Dad?" Kevin asked.

"We are your parents and will always be your parents. However, we are not your biological parents." As David O'Brien said this, Kevin shifted ever so slightly in his chair. There was no facial grimace or verbalization. Only that of a child listening intently to a person he respected, trusted, and loved.

"Who were my biological parents?" Kevin asked.

"Your biological mother had died at childbirth. You were the third of three children that were born that day. Your mother was a nurse at the delivery. She took care of you, and she fell in love with you. Your biological father was emotionally able to care for only one of the children. Two children were put up for adoption. Your mother could not bear being separated from you. That is when the decision to adopt you was made. We took you home about a week after you were born and have loved you ever since."

A tear appeared in Kevin's eye. He arose from the table, walked over to his mother first, gave her a kiss on the cheek, and followed that with hug. He then did the same with his dad. "I could not have asked for better parents," he stated in a low yet strong voice.

"Kevin," his dad continued, "I know this news comes as a shock. If you ever have questions about this, please ask us."

Kevin thought and asked, "Maybe just one. Will I ever be able to meet my brothers?"

"I don't know," his dad replied, not knowing just how involved Kevin would ultimately be in his brothers' lives.

As a child, Kevin was a colicky infant. This continued through his first decade of life. He was continually plagued by violent, incapacitating spasms of his GI tract, lasting an hour or more at a time. He would stop what he was doing, find a quiet place to lie down, and bring his knees to his chest, which always made him feel a bit better. Once they remitted, he would resume his activities, never crying and never complaining. He was always the best student in his class and the person his classmates would seek out for help. He loved football and tennis. He was voted by his teammates as captain of both teams. He also excelled scholastically and was voted the salutatorian of his high school class. At his school, this honor was not based on grades alone; it was also based on the votes of his classmates. He picked University of Michigan to play football at. He was thinking of turning pro but became fascinated by forensics during a course he took at college. He joined the police force after college.

Kevin was thirty-three when he was a rookie detective assigned to be mentored by a more senior Detective Tollins. They had just investigated the death of an elderly patient, Orin Barrow, from an apparent accidental overdose of insulin. Tollins thought the death was a simple accidental overdose. Kevin tried to reason with his more experienced mentor, Detective Tollins, the detective in charge of the homicide case, to continue the investigation.

"Just doesn't make sense. Why would a man who was injecting insulin for years make such an error? And," Kevin continued, "why would it be suicide if all pending litigation against him was settled? Also what was the mark found by the medical examiner on his neck?" Kevin asked.

Tollins was adamant. "O'Brien, this case is closed. I don't want to hear any more about it. You understand?" Beads of sweat appeared on Tollins's forehead.

Kevin felt something was not right. He also could not understand Tollins's resistance to pursue this further. He was not one to back away from injustice. He decided that he would explore this on his own, even if not sanctioned by the department and knowing full well the wrath that his partner was capable of.

An opportunity arose when his chief asked him to follow up on a break-in at the Bayside Children's Home. This would be the first case where he was the detective in charge. He was intrigued that the death of Orin Barrow, the former director of the orphanage, and the break-in at the orphanage occurred within twenty-four hours of each other and less than ten miles apart. *This could not be a coincidence,* he thought. Usually a break-in is not an exciting opportunity for a detective. Not like a murder. His chief tasked him since the department was short-staffed because of a flu bug going around. He was also the rookie detective. He jumped at the opportunity.

He called ahead to meet with the current director, Alan Presley. The director showed him around. They examined the window in the director's office and file room door that were pried open. The same way Orin Barrow's garage door was pried open. This was no coincidence. He felt for sure the same person was responsible.

Alan Presley then showed him the file room. All looked in order. No file drawers appeared to have been tampered with. Why should they? They never were locked. Out of the corner of Kevin's eye he caught a piece of paper poking out from under one of the file cabinets. He picked it up and turned it over. It was a birth certificate. "Baby Three Ludlow" was written on it. He stopped breathing for a moment, gripping the certificate tighter. He now knew the orphanage he was brought to and adopted from. He also knew that Orin Barrow knew about his birth father, and now he was dead. Could Orin Barrow's death be linked to his estranged brother, whom he knew only as Baby Two? Kevin had a nagging feeling inside that it could.

He asked Director Presley, who was standing outside the door and did not see Kevin pick up the paper from under the file cabinet, "Who is Ludlow?"

"Why do you ask?" the director responded.

"I found this birth certificate under the cabinet." Kevin showed him the certificate.

"Interesting. I don't know who that baby is, but I do know a Robert Ludlow. He was a prominent member of our community. He was chairman of Ludlow Enterprises. They called him the governor. Donated a lot to our orphanage. Probably one of the main reasons we still exist. He died recently." Kevin felt his heart skip a beat. "His son, I believe, took over the business. Robert Ludlow Jr., named after his father, but goes by Bob. Philanthropic. Not sure if this Baby Three is related, but I will check on it for you if you feel it is important."

"That would be great," Kevin answered. Kevin was sad at hearing his biological father had passed away but was at the same time ecstatic. He was on the verge of locating his long-lost brothers. He continued, "Is it usual to refer to a child as Baby Three?"

"We have children who are sent to us without knowing who the birth parents are. The hospital often records the name as John Doe or Jane Doe. However, when there are multiple babies born to a birth mother and they know the surname, but no first name has been given, the hospital can refer to them as Baby One, Baby Two, and so on. Let me check the file for this baby."

The director opened the file folder for the Ludlow babies. He continued, "We actually received both Baby Two and Baby Three Ludlow. Looks like Baby Three was adopted through a private adoption. We would have no further records on that child. Interesting that no further information about Baby Two is in this folder. That is very strange."

"Why is that?" Kevin inquired.

"We are required to keep current addresses of all children who come through the orphanage except those who have a private adoption. I don't see any information here about Baby Two, and we can't ask the prior director, Orin Barrow. He just died. Tragically, I heard. I might have another way to find the information," the director stated as he went to his Rolodex file system. "We organize records here by birth date because many of our children do not have surnames when they come to us. It is also a great way to remember when their birthdays are, so we can celebrate as a group. Not likely many children have the same birth date as Baby Two. Possibly the prior director made a separate file for Baby Two under another name. Let's see, September 16. Yup, only one child. Dexter Brunswick. I know this one," Alan Presley stated, shaking his head with obvious disapproval.

The director continued, "He aged out, meaning that he was never adopted and left the orphanage at age eighteen. I met with him several years ago. We found a trust that was set up by his father and with the prior director, Orin Barrow, as the trustee. There was no family name associated with this very intelligent young man. Admitted to medical school. But he was also an angry person."

"Angry? What do you mean?" Kevin asked.

"Well, he was not at all friendly and very ill-mannered when we spoke. I just felt he had pent-up hostility for his plight in life," the director concluded.

"Do you know where I might find him?" Kevin asked.

"Do you think he was involved in the break-in?" the director asked.

"Not sure. May be valuable for another case I am working on," Kevin stated.

"Well, here is the last address I have." The director wrote the address on a piece of paper and handed it to Kevin. "He may not be at that address now."

"Thank you. Thank you for your help. Would it be OK if I contact you if I have additional questions?"

"No problem," the director replied.

Kevin left the orphanage with more information than he could have hoped for. He was convinced Dexter Brunswick and Bob Ludlow were his estranged brothers. He also suspected that Dexter Brunswick had committed the orphanage break-in and was somehow involved in Orin Barrow's death. He just needed to find out why.

9

ALLY

The next year was a blur for Kevin. He had survived his rookie year as a detective and was partnered with his prior mentor, Detective Tollins. That was not Kevin's choice. He had tried to find Brunswick, but each time he thought he had a lead, it evaporated. He had not yet reached out to Bob Ludlow. He kept telling himself he needed to get more information before he could approach him. Then there were his girls. He had married Beth, a childhood sweetheart with long red hair. They had a beautiful baby girl whom he wanted to spend every free moment with. He also noted a change in his partner. He was more temperamental. *Problems at home,* he thought. Nonetheless, going to work was more stressful than it had been. They had been taken off several large cases simply because the chief did not want to deal with Tollins's irritable personality. This gave Kevin time to use departmental resources to locate his brothers.

It was easier locating Bob Ludlow, who was a public figure running a company, than it was Dexter Brunswick. Brunswick had moved several times since he attended medical school and residency at Yale. Brunswick never gave a forwarding address.

Bob was easy to find. Bob was thrown into the position of running a company when he was only in his midthirties. As the CEO of a multinational company, he was forever in the spotlight. Kevin read an article in the paper showcasing Bob Ludlow's accomplishments and decided it was time.

Kevin didn't know how to approach him. He felt he could not walk up to him and say, "Hey, I'm your brother." So he did what every good detective would do. He followed him. He found out that he would routinely go to a diner every Saturday morning for coffee and a muffin while he read the paper. Kevin did not know the type of person Bob was and how he would react to finding out he had a biological brother. He also did not want to freak Bob out by being followed by a detective. He decided to use the approach he was taught in his surveillance training. He would insert himself into the subject's world and daily routine. This familiarity would develop an unspoken bond between the two and ultimately a trust. He made sure that he would take a seat near where Bob would routinely sit. He did this every weekend for several months. He was waiting for the opportunity to start a discussion. The opportunity presented itself one Saturday morning. Bob had just arrived, and the waitress came over to the table.

"Hi, Bob. The regular today?" she asked.

"Yes, Mimi. And if you have a paper, please bring that along too. Mine was not delivered today," Bob stated.

Mimi was a grandma and so proud of her grandchildren, all eight. Her warm demeanor kept the customers coming back week after week. You could easily understand why her grandchildren adored her.

"Sorry, our papers have not yet arrived. Should be here soon," Mimi responded.

Overhearing this gave Kevin a chance to enter the conversation. "I have two papers. Must have delivered yours to my house," he said with a chuckle as he handed Bob the paper.

"Thank you!" Bob replied, surprised by the offer. "I've seen you here several times before. I am Bob Ludlow."

"Nice to meet you too! I'm Kevin O'Brien. Guess we have pretty much the same Saturday morning routines."

That brief encounter created a connection between them. Kevin enjoyed the brief encounters they had at the diner. In the beginning, he made a point of arriving before Bob and then, so as not to appear too obvious, he would leave before Bob started his muffin. As the weeks went by, they sometimes sat together and talked sports. Kevin got to know Bob. He liked him.

A few months later, Kevin thought it was the right time to start the discussion. They already knew a lot about each other. A trust had also been developed. Bob was fascinated about the life of a detective. They were sitting at a table in the diner across from each other, Bob with his coffee and muffin and Kevin with his egg-white omelet and a bagel. Kevin felt it was time and steered the discussion to his childhood.

Kevin opened the discussion. "I grew up not too far from here in a small town called Chester."

"I know that town!" Bob exclaimed. "Beautiful fountain right in the middle of town. Wasn't there some story about it being a wishing well?" Bob asked.

"Yes, the water was said to have healing powers thought to be imbued by the beautiful imported Australian rainforest jasper stones that they embedded in the walls of the well," Kevin said. "Folklore had it that those of pure heart would be granted their wish if they toss a coin in the well while making a wish. I would spend hours at a time, and many pennies, when I was young, hoping my wishes would come true."

"No kidding. What did you wish for?" Bob asked.

This was the opportunity Kevin was looking for. "I found out at the age of fourteen that I was adopted. I had great parents, but I could not stop thinking why. Why didn't my biological parents want me? That's when I started going to the wishing well. I wished for the answer," Kevin said in an almost apologetic, soft voice.

"And did you get an answer?" Bob asked.

"Well, I had this case that brought me to the Bayside Children's home," Kevin responded.

"Very familiar with that place. My family has supported them for many years. Were you adopted through there?" Bob asked.

Kevin did not know how Bob would react to what he had to say. But he had to say it anyway.

"I was," Kevin replied. "My mother had died during my birth. What I learned in my visit to the orphanage was that my birth father's last name was Ludlow." Kevin looked directly at Bob, waiting for his reaction. It seemed to him to be an eternity when, in fact, it was only seconds.

"Whoa!" Bob exclaimed. "Are we related?"

"I don't know." Kevin replied. "But I would like to find out. I must confess. I first came to this diner to meet you but didn't know how to start the conversation. But with the brief encounters we had, I felt a connection between us. Something difficult to express in words."

"Strange, I had the same reaction," Bob replied.

"There is also one more thing I found out," Kevin said.

"And what is that?" Bob asked.

"I was Baby Three. There were two other children born to the Ludlows that day," Kevin stated.

"Wow!" Bob responded. "There could be three of us?"

Bob could have reacted very differently. But something inside him knew this could be what he felt was missing from his life. His father never spoke about his family. He only found out that he had an uncle at his father's funeral. He had no idea if there were other family members.

However, Bob's practical side, and the detective in Kevin, needed to confirm the possibility. They both agreed to go together for sibling DNA testing. Identical twins share 100 percent of their DNA, while full siblings, also known as first-degree relatives, share 50 percent of their DNA. Half siblings, or second-degree relatives, share 25 percent of their DNA. Always better to have a parent's DNA to test it against. But unfortunately, this was not available, since both potential parents had died.

Bob had the contacts. He reached out to his physician friend, who wrote the order for him. Kevin was not as well connected. He had to make an appointment with his physician and pay the fee for a consultation. Only then was he given the handwritten prescription to take to the lab. They both met at the lab. A new one had just opened for this genetic testing. The field of genetics was in its infancy. The Nobel prize in physiology and medicine was awarded in 1962 to Watson, Crick, and Wilkins for their discovery of the molecular structure of nucleic acids, which are the building blocks of DNA. The field started expanding. However, the clinical applications, including paternity and sibling testing, were more recent developments. A small local company, ReproMed, was among the first to offer this testing and had opened a lab in Stanford. The ReproMed lab was one of the few labs around for testing. Bob and Kevin made an appointment to go together for blood testing.

It took several weeks for the results to return. Bob and Kevin shared more than 50 percent of genes in common, making them full siblings.

Bob and Kevin celebrated their finding each other by meeting for beers at a local pub. They met, they hugged, they talked, and they drank.

"So," Bob asked, "why didn't just come over to me at the diner initially and tell me your suspicion? Why did you wait months?"

"Didn't know how you would respond. This was too important to me. Too important to both of us. If I scared you off because you thought I was just some crazy person, I would have lost the opportunity to find out. Besides, I needed to know the type of person you were. Guess it was the detective in me," Kevin responded.

"Amazing. Just can't believe I have found a brother!" Bob exclaimed.

"Neither can I," Kevin agreed, his voice now returning to a softer and more somber tone. "However, there is one more bit of information I have not yet told you. Something that you might not be too comfortable with," Kevin stated.

"What's that?" Bob asked.

"It is about who I believe is the third sibling. What started my quest for you was that I was involved in two cases. One concerned the death of a man who was thought to have overdosed on his insulin, and the other was a break-in at an orphanage. Not just any orphanage—the Bayside Children's Home," Kevin stated.

"And you think they are related?" Bob asked.

"Yes. I am sure of it. But the worst part is that our other brother, who goes by the name Dexter Brunswick, I believe committed these two crimes and is looking for us," Kevin declared.

"Wow. That is a shocker. I just received a call from his office to make an appointment. My wife, Debra, and I have been having some problems having a child, and his office contacted us to make an appointment. I was surprised to hear from them, since we never contacted his office. Do you think he knows I am his brother? How did he get our number, and what does he want?" Bob asked.

"From what I could surmise from my interview with the director at the orphanage, Dexter seemed to be a troubled and angry man. He was maligned by the prior director, the staff, and other orphans. He had attacked and seriously injured another orphan when he was only six without any signs of remorse. And, I feel he might have been involved in the death of Orin Barrow, the prior director of the orphanage. Possibly he feels it is revenge for what he sees as injustices that happened to him. Or he wants to find his family, who he feels was torn away from him. Or possibly he sees us as having avoided his plight and now wants to make us feel the pain he had. Whatever it is, we need to find out." Kevin said.

"Even if he did all that, and right now it is only a supposition, he is still our brother. Don't we have an obligation to help him? Isn't that what families do?" Bob continued. "There is no proof that he killed anyone. A feeling is certainly not proof of a crime. And, the injury sustained by the other orphan could have been an accident. I know I just found he might be a brother, but hell, I just found out you and I are related too! Family is everything to me. I need to reach out to him. We need to reach out to him. You said he was mistreated in the orphanage. He is probably hurting."

"You make great points. I agree with your commitment to family. However, I'm very troubled by what I have heard about him. We need to be careful." Kevin responded.

10

COERCION

Tuesday, February 4, 1992

Polyzygotic siblings who grew up apart from one another—like the Ludlow triplets—develop unique personalities. Studies have demonstrated that siblings separated at birth are influenced by many factors, genetic and nongenetic, that determine their behavior; it's reminiscent of the old nature-versus-nurture debate. Social psychologists studying these factors call this the cohort effect. This was certainly true for the three Ludlow offspring. Bob was the enterprising intellectual, Kevin the compassionate investigator, and Dexter the avenging malevolent.

What Bob and Kevin did not know was that Brunswick had started ReproMed as an outgrowth of his interest in genetics, which had begun in medical school. He particularly was interested in what genetic sequences were responsible for sperm production in men. He wanted to know how to interfere with this process. His team thought that he was trying to produce a male contraceptive. But his motivation was more sinister.

Something irreversibly changed in him when he mercilessly attacked the eight-year-old who had called him "devil's child" on the orphanage playground. He became self-absorbed with a complete lack of empathy for others. His narcissistic personality fueled all that he did. It likely contributed to his significant academic achievements but also drove his malevolence. He was focused on payback. In some twisted way, he wanted others who he felt maligned him to feel his pain. That unfortunate group included those at the orphanage as well as his family, who he felt abandoned him. It also extended to his patients and those he felt were threats to his goal of gaining singular recognition for his academic achievements. That included Barry Gifford. He knew that Barry was working on similar research. He had also searched the hospital database and found out that Donald Gifford was a patient at the hospital. He had found a billing entry for a semen analysis. *Could it be that Donald and his wife had difficulty conceiving? Could it be that Donald was his biological father's brother and that Barry was the third Ludlow child?* He thought that would make sense. Ludlow would have his brother, who was having difficulty conceiving, adopt Barry. Possibly the adoption caused the brothers to drift apart. Brunswick was convinced that was the case. He needed to get someone to get close to Barry to prove it. He also needed to learn more about Barry and his work. He needed someone on the inside.

Brunswick had made alliances with several local labs under the guise that the information obtained was part of a university-approved research study. He wanted to be alerted to any patients presenting with azoospermia, a condition where no sperm are found in the ejaculate. He would then have his office contact the patient to have him come in for evaluation and blood genetic testing. He knew that these patients would be the group who would most quickly lead him to his goal. He had already sequenced his own DNA and was looking for similarities in others.

Brunswick was also notified when a specific genetic sequence involving the NR5A1 gene was found in any of ReproMed's clients. He received an alert for Bob Ludlow. The information he received was limited, however. He received only the specific sequence of interest together with the patient's name and address. He did not receive an alert for Kevin. Kevin either did not have the specific sequence, or if he did, his variant was not detected by the test. He also did not receive the reason why testing was being performed or the other person being tested. That was a fateful omission.

Brunswick was drinking a cup of coffee when he received the alert. His hands began shaking. Coffee spilled freely on the floor. He had found a match to a specific sequence in his DNA. He had found a brother. He asked his office staff to find out more about Bob. He learned that Bob Ludlow was wealthy and had lived a privileged life. Not a life of abuse and rejection like his. "Damn!" he screamed out loud, not caring if others heard him. He needed to meet him. Indeed, he wanted something from him.

Coincidently at the same time, he was alerted that Bob's semen analysis demonstrated azoospermia. He had his staff contact Bob and arrange for a consultation. The appointment was set for a Monday morning. Each knew that the other was his brother. Bob, although apprehensive, needed to learn more about Dexter. He was steadfast in his commitment to family. He accepted the appointment and let Kevin know.

Brunswick's medical office was on the first floor of a nondescript two-story medical office building less than a mile from Metropolitan University Hospital. It was a large office space with two consultation rooms, a procedure room, and a laboratory. The waiting room had the standard commercial photographs in metal frames. The walls were painted white with a drop-down ceiling and fluorescent lights. There were functional office chairs separated by tables with a few magazines and a small Plexiglas stand that held brochures extolling the accomplishments of Dr. Dexter Brunswick. The receptionist was a meticulously dressed woman in her forties with her hair in a bun and glasses. She greeted Bob and Debra as they entered. Although Bob discussed meeting Kevin with Debra, he had not yet told her of what Kevin had told him about Dr. Brunswick's possible dark past.

Bob walked in with Debra at his side. "Hi, I am Bob Ludlow. I am here for my appointment with Dr. Brunswick."

The receptionist responded perfunctorily without looking up from her computer. "Mr. Ludlow, please complete these papers and return them to me." She handed him a stack of questionnaires and releases to complete and sign.

Bob was already feeling uneasy about being there. The decor and the receptionist's attitude did not help. He let it go, thinking she was just having a bad day. He completed the forms quickly. He then signed the customary disclaimers and returned them to the receptionist.

"Dr. Brunswick will be with you shortly," she brusquely replied.

Although Bob and Debra were surprised by the receptionist's manner, they were pleased to be taken so promptly after he had returned the papers. He was brought into a room where a medical assistant took his weight and vitals while Debra sat with him. The assistant was a pleasant young woman in her midtwenties. He asked her, "Have you been working here long?"

She was uninhibited in her response. "This is my first week at this office. I was sent from an agency. From what I heard, the doctor goes through medical assistants weekly. I have very few dealings with him. Just know he wants things done his way. I received a twenty-page packet to read over before I could start. I was also required to sign a confidentiality agreement. No matter. I am going back to school in two weeks. Just need this job to get some spending money."

The perky and chatty coed completed her tasks and left the exam room to enter the information into the computer records. A more stoic male physician's assistant entered and performed a physical exam and drew blood for testing. Very little was said. Bob assumed this was by protocol. He then was taken for several ultrasound exams and brought back into the exam room by the PA.

"The doctor will be with you shortly," he stated as he left the room.

Again, the same words the receptionist used. *Rehearsed,* Bob thought.

Bob was anxious waiting for Dexter Brunswick, his estranged brother, to enter the room. He was unsure how he would react or feel in response to seeing, for the first time, a brother he was separated from since birth. Kevin's words of caution echoed in his mind. He would not have to wait long.

The door to the room opened. A man, an inch or so taller than Bob, with a goatee entered. Brunswick's physique was surprisingly like Bob's. He kept his weight under good control.

"I am Dr. Brunswick. You are Bob Ludlow?" Brunswick asked with eyes fixated on the chart. Bob stared at this man. He could not find the words to answer this simple question. Brunswick looked at Bob, not hearing an answer. Brunswick's blue eyes pierced into his soul. Bob found the words.

"Yes, yes, I am Bob Ludlow." Then he added, "This is my wife, Debra."

Brunswick made no attempt to make eye contact with Debra. Nor did he acknowledge her presence. *Weird*, both Bob and Debra thought.

"I understand that you have been unsuccessfully trying to have a baby, and your semen analysis demonstrated no sperm. Is that correct?" Brunswick asked with very little inflection in his voice.

"That's correct," Bob answered.

"Do you have any brothers?" Brunswick asked. Bob was curious at Brunswick's choice of words. He did not ask if he had any siblings—rather if he had a brother. *Did he know about Kevin?* Bob did not want to lie, thinking that Brunswick might detect that. Instead, he would take a middle road.

"I might have. I was separated from a sibling at birth," Bob said. "I don't know if the sibling is a brother or sister. I have been searching for him or her."

"Any luck?" Brunswick asked.

"Not yet," Bob responded. That seemed to pacify Brunswick. At least for now.

Brunswick said very little as he conducted a brief physical exam. Bob was impressed by Brunswick's strong grip when taking his blood pressure. He obviously worked out. He then stated, "I will await the results of the blood tests and then see you back in two weeks when the tests return to discuss what needs to be done."

What needs to be done? Bob thought. *Don't I get a say in that?* He wanted to respond but held it back. The appointment was over.

Two weeks passed quickly. He had relayed his experience at the appointment to Kevin, who again cautioned Bob to be careful.

The follow-up appointment was again on a Monday morning. He entered the office with Debra, who reluctantly accompanied him. She had felt so uncomfortable during the prior visit. To their surprise, this time they were greeted with a smile from the receptionist and brought immediately into Brunswick's office.

Brunswick was almost beaming. What a change from the first visit, they both thought. He greeted them, looking at both directly in the eyes. In fact, almost darting from one to the other. *A bit of mania*, they thought. But certainly, a welcome change.

Brunswick began the conversation. "I have good news!" he exclaimed. "I believe I can find out what is preventing your sperm from coming out and help you have a baby."

"That is great news. What did the blood tests show?" he inquired.

"That your hormones are being suppressed. To find out exactly what is suppressing them, I will need to do a testis biopsy. The biopsy is a simple outpatient procedure. We can do it on Friday. Also, if a blockage is found, I would try to reconnect the tubes so that sperm can come out in the ejaculate."

Bob and Debra turned to each other and smiled. They were elated by the news and more so by the change in Brunswick's demeanor.

"Is there any danger to having the procedure?" Bob asked.

Brunswick became serious. "There are always possibilities, with any procedure, that complications can occur. With this procedure bleeding, infection, and anesthesia risks are all possible. But not likely. There is also the possibility of loss of the testis, although that is very unlikely."

Bob looked at Debra. She so much wanted to have a child. She did not know about Kevin's concerns. Bob kept telling himself that they were just suspicions and not proven. They agreed to have Brunswick do the procedure on Friday.

Bob had to go for preoperative blood work that day. He also made an appointment for the CT scan that Brunswick ordered. He met with Kevin that Wednesday.

"Still going through with the procedure?" Kevin asked.

"Yes. At our last meeting Dr. Brunswick was very different. Actually, pleasant and encouraging. And, I could not let Debra down. Besides it is only a testis biopsy." Bob replied as if trying to convince himself.

"I don't want to cause you more concern. I can understand the stress you and Debra are already under. I just don't want any harm coming to you." Kevin said apologetically.

"I understand and appreciate your concern." Bob said. He also thought, *My brother wouldn't hurt me.*

The day of surgery came quickly. Debra brought Bob to the ambulatory surgery center the morning of surgery. Bob was compliant in not eating or drinking since midnight. He was both hungry and thirsty.

Brunswick arrived about fifteen minutes prior to surgery. He brought a large briefcase with him. *Guess he's going to do work between cases,* Bob thought.

"Have any questions about the procedure before I ask you to sign the consent?" Brunswick asked.

Bob looked at the consent, which stated the procedure as an excisional biopsy of the testis or testes and possible ductal reconstruction. "Just one. How large a sample is taken?" Bob asked.

"It actually depends on the size of the testis. Although a biopsy is small, about the size of a pea, it sometimes amounts to a larger proportion of the testis, especially if the testis is small. As in your case," Brunswick replied.

It sounded reasonable to Bob, and he had faith in his brother, so he signed the consent. Debra went to the surgical waiting area as Bob was brought into the operating room.

The procedure took about thirty minutes. Bob was wheeled into the recovery room. When he awoke, Debra was brought into the recovery room to sit with him. Bob asked her how the procedure went. Debra's eyes were red. Tears had made her eyeliner run. He knew something was not right. "Debra?" he asked.

"Dr. Brunswick told me that your right testis was so small that most of it was taken for the biopsy. He said that you would be fine and that the left testis, which he did not biopsy, would work in its place," Debra said, sobbing.

"OK. Not so bad," Bob said. "Why are you crying?"

"He said we would not be able to have children. He said you had no sperm production," Debra answered with her words broken by her crying. Bob was awake enough to wonder how Dr. Brunswick could know that there was no sperm production without waiting for the pathology results to return. He also was distraught that he made Debra so upset.

Over the next two weeks, Bob recovered from his procedure. To him it was a minor procedure. The scrotal swelling dissipated. He felt no real difference with the loss of his right testis. He was patiently awaiting the appointment with Dr. Brunswick to go over the results of pathology report and his treatment options. Bob was very concerned about Debra. She had been extremely quiet since the procedure. He found her sobbing on several occasions. She would quickly compose herself when she heard Bob approaching.

They entered the reception area, and Debra tightly gripped Bob's arm. They were quickly brought into Dr. Brunswick's office, and they sat in front of his desk. Brunswick looked up from his papers.

Looking at Bob, Brunswick asked, "How are you feeling today?"

"Not bad," Bob replied. He did have a bit of discomfort but was not the type to admit to it.

"Well, I have the results of your biopsy." Brunswick paused and then stated matter-of-factly, "Unfortunately, findings don't bode well for your future fertility."

Debra could not contain her emotions. Bob was crushed, but he had to be strong for Debra. Bob moved his chair right next to her, so he could put his arm around her. Brunswick was not exactly truthful in his statement. He knew it. He also knew how to manipulate people and what he wanted. He waited for Bob to ask the question.

"There must be something that can be done. Some new research or experimental treatment?" Bob inquired.

Brunswick had his opening and he took it. "There is some work being done by a colleague of mine, a Dr. Barry Gifford, on stimulating sperm production in testes like yours." Calling Barry a colleague was also far from the truth. Brunswick continued, "He is giving a lecture at the Gottersman Research Pavilion opening ceremony at the hospital next week. You might want to attend to hear what he says and decide if you would like to consult with him."

Bob looked at Debra, as did Brunswick. Hearing of possible hope, she could compose herself. Bob knew that he had to pursue this opportunity. He would do anything for Debra. Brunswick knew he had his spy.

11

DECEPTION

When I first saw Bob and Debra in consultation, Bob was my age, approaching thirty-seven, and Debra was three years his junior. At thirty-four, she was approaching the age when conceiving was a primary concern. She knew that over the next five years her fertility would certainly decrease. She had the imperative that it was now or never. The biological clock was ticking. It was the possibility of never that scared her. They filled me in on their journey in trying to conceive. Bob had met with Dr. Brunswick a year or so prior. Bob first saw Dr. Brunswick for infertility. How he got to see Dr. Brunswick was intriguing. He and Debra had been trying to conceive for two years. She had been seen by Dr. Daniel Rothberg, a world-renowned reproductive endocrinologist. They underwent a barrage of the usual tests, which often seemed more a test of one's commitment to having a child than of one's ability to have a child.

Medicine was paternalistic. There was no shared decision making. Many doctors often told you what to do and what tests you needed with little explanation. Dutiful patients followed the doctor's orders, often enduring humiliating and painful tests. But what was most frustrating was the dearth of information that doctors provided about what these tests showed. Fortunately, Dan Rothberg was a very different kind of doctor. He wanted Debra to know exactly what was found. He explained to her that the blood studies that evaluated the pituitary's control over her ovaries were normal. An X-ray study that evaluated the pathway of the egg to the uterus along the fallopian tubes was also normal. An endometrial biopsy found that the lining of her uterus was normal at the time of ovulation, and a pelvic sonogram confirmed what the blood studies suggested—that she ovulated normally.

Debra mentioned that these normal results were comforting to her. She had been worried about the results. She stated that she had vivid memories about being pregnant several years prior with her first husband. She had lost the unborn child in an automobile accident that also took the life of her husband. It had happened so quickly. They had been driving upstate in their four-wheel-drive vehicle to go skiing at their favorite Vermont resort. A storm started. The temperature was five degrees below freezing, and rain on the road was beginning to freeze. Her husband was driving on the edge of a fifty-foot ravine. There might have been a deer or a tree branch in the road. Attempting to avoid it, he lost control. He had no chance to regain control as the car slid on the ice. It rolled sideways down the ravine, flipping once. Her husband was crushed and killed instantly. Debra was saved by the airbag. Unfortunately, the blunt trauma to her abdomen ruptured her placenta, causing internal bleeding and loss of her fetus. It took a long time for her to accept her husband's death and the death of her unborn baby. One probably never completely gets over such a tragedy.

With these normal results, Dr. Rothberg suggested that Bob obtain a semen analysis. He was referred to the lab at the university. Bob made an appointment for the next morning. He received an e-mail almost immediately with a link to a secure website to enter information for his proper identification in anticipation of the sample he was to give the next morning. Although he felt a bit uncomfortable providing some of the more personal information, he complied.

Upon arriving at the lab, he needed only to sign the sheets that were printed out with information about the time the specimen was given and the number of days of abstinence. He was then asked to confirm the information on the label that was affixed to his specimen container and then to produce the specimen. He felt this was quite efficient, and although he still felt embarrassed, the efficiency throughout the process put him more at ease. The results, however, were disturbing.

He received a call from Dr. Rothberg that evening. There were no sperm in the sample. Not even one. Dr. Rothberg had referred him to several male fertility specialists but not Dr. Brunswick. However, almost minutes after he got off the phone with Dr. Rothberg, he received a call from Dr. Brunswick's office, asking if he would like to make an appointment. When he inquired how they got his number, the secretary stated that Dr. Brunswick had spoken with Dr. Rothberg, who suggested they call. It sounded plausible to him, so he made the appointment.

It wasn't until his experience with Dr. Brunswick that he sought a second opinion and found out from Dr. Rothberg that he had not referred Dr. Brunswick and hadn't given his phone number to Dr. Brunswick. No one knew how Brunswick got his number or how he even knew to call him.

When I first saw Bob Ludlow in consultation, I had no idea what I was about to uncover. Apparently neither did he, even though Dr. Brunswick had previously evaluated and operated on him.

I tried to not let my concerns about Dr. Brunswick cloud my evaluation of Bob. Bob continued to recount his evaluation and treatment with Dr. Brunswick, so I could know what had been done and what data had already been obtained.

"I was nervous when I first consulted with Dr. Brunswick." Bob admitted. "I had many questions that I wanted to ask. What did the absence of sperm mean? Would I be able to have children? I was also worried that other, more dangerous, conditions might be present. I had no idea if these conditions could be fixed."

These were typical concerns that many of my patients had. However, it appeared that Bob's questions were not answered.

Bob continued. "A medical assistant then took my medical history and then my blood pressure. A physician's assistant then entered the exam room to examine me and take blood tests. I then underwent several ultrasound imaging exams. Only then did Dr. Brunswick see me. Dr. Brunswick asked me a few questions that his assistants had already asked but never discussed his findings or suspicions. He also did not discuss with me what the finding of the lack of sperm in the ejaculate could mean or if he could help me. He just stated that he would see him back in a few weeks when the blood tests returned. Looking back, It was probably my fault for not asking the questions that were on my mind. I guess I just thought that this was the way things were done, so I went along with the plan."

It was puzzling to me that Bob, a brilliant businessman, was so accepting of his impersonalized treatment. It was equally unsettling how some people became doctors without even the slightest bit of compassion. Was this a case of nurture or nature? Not all parents teach their children to have empathy. It's certainly not something they teach in medical school. It's something you either have or you don't. This attribute was even more important in this age of managed care where patients became "lives" and doctors became "health-care providers." There appears never to be enough time to spend with patients whose questions become more numerous and complicated as medicine becomes more technological with a multiplicity of treatment options available.

Dr. Brunswick was evidently not a compassionate man. Other factors appeared to motivate him. Whether they were related to finances, status, or avarice, only he knew. From Bob's point of view, he had an obvious lack of concern for his patients. Why was Bob so apathetic when it came to Dr. Brunswick's uncaring attitude? It was not at all what one would expect of a high-powered executive.

Colleagues had told me that Dr. Brunswick was always a difficult person, but he turned downright despicable about ten years ago. He became preoccupied with starting a research company involved with the genetic engineering of fertility drugs. He had never married. In fact, no one ever saw him date. He was a man with a mission. However, no one could figure out what that mission was. I had been asked by the hospital administrator to head up a committee to raise money to help defray the cost of fertility treatments for financially challenged patients. Brunswick never participated in any hospital fund-raising events.

My interactions with Dr. Brunswick were strained. He would often walk past me in the hospital without acknowledging my presence. Whether it was a public comment made at presentations I gave or as a letter to the editor written in response to a paper I had published, his remarks were always critical. I assumed that he was an unhappy person who viewed me as his competition. I had approached him several times to try to make a truce, but he was unwavering. With his ice-cold dirty-blue eyes and curt reply, he would deny it all.

I remembered that on my initial physical examination, Bob had a solitary left testis and no sperm in his semen specimen. There was a healed incision in his right lower abdomen. He was missing a right testis. This was consistent with the operative report that stated the right testis had been removed.

After the physical examination, I spent more than an hour with Bob, trying to both win his confidence and repair his self-esteem. He was easy to talk to and very interested in learning. He would ask great questions and listen intently as I responded. Even when I went into a pedagogical rant, he would patiently listen, occasionally and politely interjecting a question to get me back on track. Bob was fully masculinized and had been reared as a male since birth. He had no questions about his masculinity until Dr. Brunswick's callous remarks and inappropriate surgery.

When I measured his hormones, I found an extremely high level of estrogen, a female hormone, and a low level of testosterone, the major male hormone, together with a decreased level of the pituitary hormones that control the production of testosterone and sperm production, LH and FSH. This didn't make sense. In a man, estrogen is formed primarily when the enzyme aromatase converts testosterone to estrogen. But his testosterone was low, which would preclude a large amount of estrogen being formed this way. I wondered what could have caused this. A tumor of the testis-producing estrogen? Or possibly the adrenal glands or liver producing excess estrogen? This was a fascinating patient! I needed to repeat these tests to make sure they were right and find out if Dr. Brunswick had done any more testing. I also needed to see a copy of his records. I immediately sent over a signed release for medical information form and requested the records. It took many calls from my office and several calls from Bob before only a few pages of his medical records were received.

It appeared from Bob's records that Dr. Brunswick had been so consumed with his own agenda that the moment Bob walked into his office, he scheduled Bob for an operation to "biopsy the testes and possibly open up a blockage." Without the completion of a prudent workup, he presumably thought that the lack of sperm in Bob's ejaculate was because of an obstruction of the tubes carrying sperm from the testes. It was interesting that genetic testing was not part of his evaluation since a patient may not produce sperm because of an abnormality in the number of chromosomes. Also lacking from the records were the results of ultrasound testing and a request for additional imaging. These tests might have identified abnormalities in Bob's reproductive organs, which could possibly account for the lack of sperm. Some abnormalities could have been found on an exam also. However, the only exam report was the physician's assistant's perfunctory note. The records that I had did not support the procedure that was performed and conspicuously lacked the necessary data to go forward with surgery.

From the notes in Bob's chart, it appeared that when the findings at the time of surgery failed to show a blockage, Brunswick removed one of Bob's testes, stating that "the blood supply to the testis was compromised." He was just "preventing further complications," his note added. He requested a CT scan, but the results were not back before the surgery was performed. This was all backward. It didn't make sense. A CT scan often gives the surgeon valuable information about what is present, absent, and possibly abnormal. It serves as a road map for surgery. It should have been reviewed prior to surgery and not as an afterthought.

This was not the first time I had found Dr. Brunswick so irresponsible in his medical care. I remembered when he had performed several inappropriate invasive urologic procedures on a patient with polycystic kidney disease—a disease in which the kidney is susceptible to life-threating infections. Each of these procedures might easily have caused an infection. Given Bob's anatomy—which Dr. Brunswick appeared to never evaluate prior to surgery—the procedure he performed on Bob just didn't make sense.

I recalled the monthly hospital conference at which medical errors were discussed. Other urologists had questioned Dr. Brunswick about his perfunctory physical examination. At best, these procedures were considered experimental, and they often resulted in patient disfigurement and bad outcomes that led to a multitude of lawsuits. Considering this, I had always wondered how he was able to continue to practice.

I had also heard through the grapevine that Dr. Brunswick had built his research facility with private monies obtained from his cronies. That should be cause for concern since many of the donors were trustees for the hospital. At that time, I didn't know about hospital politics and the lure of research dollars. I began to understand more recently how the system really worked.

12

RECORDS

I finally received Bob's CT scan and asked my staff to arrange a follow-up consultation with him and Debra to go over the results and discuss treatment options. This was not something I wanted to do by phone. I wanted to get all records together prior to our meeting so I could show them the data while explaining my thoughts to Bob and Debra. They needed to know the truth. Something Brunswick couldn't—or wouldn't—provide them.

My office was on the ninth floor of the Faculty Practice Building across the courtyard from the hospital. We referred to Metropolitan University Hospital as MUH or jokingly as the white elephant because of its immense size and white color. It was, in fact, an architectural gem. The monumental building complex was inspired by a fourteenth-century palace with Gothic touches and rose over twenty stories. With a squash court on top to boot! The same architect designed the Faculty Practice Building, although it was more modest in size and detail. My office location was ideal with the clinic area adjacent to my office. My research laboratory was on the floor directly below. It was also only a short walk across an enclosed bridge to the in-patient hospital facility. My predecessor left me a large wooden desk that dated back over fifty years. I had moved it so that I could look out of the two ten-foot windows in my office above the courtyard. The panes of glass were encased with the soot that seemed to cover everything in the city, but they still allowed sunlight to enter the office. My office was a place where I could concentrate as well as place to see patients away from the frenzied environment of the city. I had two large lightboxes, a relic of days gone by, when the only way films could be viewed was to place them in the clips of these boxes and have the light illuminate them. Most images were now digitalized and easily viewed on a computer. These lightboxes came in handy when the copies of Bob's CT scan were delivered.

The CT scan was remarkable in the information it provided. The fact that Bob initially had two testes in and of itself was reportable. But the results of the CT scan were even more incredible. Not only had Bob had two testes, but he also had two ovaries and a uterus. A true hermaphrodite—a one-of-a-kind case! Nonetheless, Dr. Brunswick never informed Bob of the CT findings, at least not these remarkable findings. Bob had only remembered that Brunswick said he had "no chance of ever fathering a child and that he needed an operation that would leave him with no testes." This vile man had removed a testicle for no apparent reason, and then he had begun to dismember Bob's psyche. It appeared he was planning to continue to do the same to his body. It was after Brunswick brought up my name that he thought of seeing me for a second opinion. However, it was Bob's brother-in-law, Dr. Mark Niebling, who pushed him into seeing me for a second opinion.

Mark was a physician from the old school. He was trained as a general practitioner back in the sixties when medicine was less dependent on technology and more dependent on trust. In his day, doctors were respected. There was no need for malpractice insurance since a patient would never consider suing a physician. Well, times had certainly changed. Mark had retired several years ago, in large part because of a lawsuit brought against him by the son of a longtime patient of his, Mary Ellen Kane. His first lawsuit in almost forty years of practice. Mary Ellen had died after a long and difficult course with gastric cancer. He had known her most of his career. He had even driven to her house in the blizzard of 1977 after she had called him in despair when the ambulance ran off the road and got stuck in a snowdrift. There was already four feet of snow on the ground. Mary Ellen was in active labor with her first child, Bill. It took him over an hour to make the trip that usually took less than ten minutes. He delivered Bill when the ambulance was unable to reach the house. He had cared for all her children, often without charge, since Mary Ellen's husband was ill and frequently without work. Yet with all this, her son filed suit against him, stating that he had "abandoned" her during her battle with gastric cancer. What an absurdity. Nothing could be further from the truth, but Bill saw Mark's position as a physician as a potential source of easy money. This action so embittered Mark that he became deeply depressed and soon decided to leave the profession rather than deal with this new demeaning attitude toward physicians.

What I couldn't understand was why Dr. Brunswick seemed to have so little concern for Bob Ludlow as a patient. He seemed to be treating Bob as a subject in an experiment instead of a patient with real concerns. But what was he searching for? In his brief operative note—a paragraph that surgeons or their delegates must write in the patient's chart before leaving the operating room—Dr. Brunswick stated that he had found a tumor in one of Bob's testes and removed it. The word tumor can mean almost anything from a benign cyst to a cancerous mass. I couldn't find any imaging study to confirm his finding.

A testis tumor is usually first identified through an ultrasound. Although a CT scan or MRI could also show a tumor, an ultrasound is the most common and often the only imaging study that is performed for the diagnosis of testis cancer. Without an ultrasound showing a tumor, a surgeon would not have any indication to operate. What happened to the ultrasound that Bob reported he had? Did Brunswick disregard the findings and make the report disappear? Did he know it contradicted what he stated he found at surgery? I needed to see the pathology report to see what was removed at surgery. However, as I would soon discover, that was not going to be easy.

I first tried accessing the report through the computerized information service by entering Bob's full name and date of birth. When that didn't work, I entered his medical record number. Still no luck. I then tried to access it through my patient list. Unfortunately, the system wouldn't accept my access ID since it wasn't yet tied to Bob's records. The only way to obtain the report would be directly from the pathology department. I decided to walk the four floors down to the fifth floor.

I entered the fifth-floor pathology office. Ann Sawyer was at the reception desk.

"Hi, Ann. How's the day been?"

"Dr. Gifford, what can I do for you?" Ann said as she continued typing a report.

I could always tell when Ann was in a foul mood. She would barely respond to questions, or she'd be curt in her response and would never look you in the eyes. "I was looking for a path report on a patient of mine. A Bob Ludlow, medical record number five-six-one-four-three-eight." A pause followed and a soft, yet perceptible, exasperated sigh.

"Just one moment," she replied as she typed it into her terminal. "Sorry, the report is unavailable."

"What do you mean unavailable? I know the surgery was quite some time ago."

"The file only specifies an accession number without a report. It could have been misfiled."

"Misfiled? Isn't that unusual with an electronic retrieval system?" I asked in disbelief.

"I'll have to ask my supervisor if she knows where it could be. Unfortunately, she's away on vacation and won't be back until next week."

I couldn't believe what I was hearing. It didn't make sense. The report had to be somewhere. In this day and age, reports not dictated within ten days of surgery resulted in a physician's administrative suspension. This would make a doctor unable to book cases, admit patients, or in the case of a surgical pathologist, jeopardize their incentive bonus. Misfiled? Could it have been deleted from the system, possibly intentionally? I couldn't believe the pathology department would be so careless with their records.

I couldn't wait. I headed down the hall into Bert Evers's office. Bert was a brilliant man: first in his medical school class at Johns Hopkins and a perfectionist. As chairman of the surgical pathology department, he would never stand for this.

After apologizing profusely to Bert for taking up his time with such a mundane matter, I explained to him my dilemma and the difficulty in finding the report. As I expected, he was furious at his secretarial staff members, who were responsible for assuring studies were completed on time and readily available for review.

"Damn these incompetents. I should fire the whole bunch. Unfortunately, I'd have the union on my back. I'll get that report to you today," Bert promised.

I took the elevator back to the ninth floor.

Somehow, after a phone call from the chairman to the department administrator, the report was suddenly found. I received a copy to my secure hospital e-mail from Bert. The pathology report stated that only a "small section of the right testicle was received and was completely sectioned." My throat tightened. A small section? Bob was missing his entire right testis. The report went on. "The biopsy was found to consist of seminiferous tubules with hypospermatogenesis." This was a term that pathologists used to describe decreased sperm production of the testes in subfertile men. The pathologist hadn't seen a tumor, but he or she knew everything wasn't perfect. The report did not specify whether mature sperm were found.

I wondered what this meant. If mature sperm were present in the testis, why weren't they found in the ejaculate? Was Dr. Brunswick correct in assuming that Bob had a blockage preventing sperm from coming out, or was it that the maturation of sperm stopped before mature sperm were formed? I needed to see the slides for myself. I still could not understand why the operative report stated that the right testis was removed when the pathology report clearly stated that a small right testis biopsy, "measuring 0.5 cm by 0.8 cm by 0.7 cm, less than 1/30 the size of a normal testis, was received." What happened to the rest of the testis? It clearly was not there on my examination. In addition, there was no ultrasound report prior to surgery that documented the presence of a testicular tumor—which is standard practice in the diagnosis of a testicular mass. The pathologist's report also didn't discuss a tumor. Only Dr. Brunswick's notes from his examination stated there was a tumor. I needed to see the nurse's notes from the operating room. The nurses could always be counted on to write down the details. Their notes were required to document the procedure and all tissues that were removed. I went back to the hospital chart and found the operating room notes dutifully written by the circulating nurse. The nurse who is not scrubbed in to the case is called the circulating nurse. He or she has the responsibility for logging the chronology of the procedure such as when the patient arrived in the room, when the "time-out" started and ended, the time the anesthesiologist stated the patient was ready for the surgeon to proceed with the procedure, a.k.a. release time. The circulating nurse also itemized all supplies used and of course all tissues removed from the patient and their disposition. Clearly in the record was "small section of the right testis sent to pathology." Then, almost as an afterthought, since it was written with a thicker pen, "orchiectomy specimen taken personally by Dr. Brunswick to the lab." A specimen the lab had not received.

Male fertility, in particular abnormalities of the development of the male genitalia, fascinated me. The reproductive potential of true hermaphrodites therefore was of great interest. Prior work from an Israeli group had suggested that sperm production in the testes of true hermaphrodites was suppressed by a substance that they partially characterized, but by what and from where this substance was secreted was unknown. Over the past several years, I had been working on this question in the hope of developing a male contraceptive.

One of the great pleasures of being part of an academic institution was to give lectures to first-year medical students. These energetic and talented students just wanted to learn. The politics of medicine had not tainted them. Everyone who lectured in medical school was assigned a set of lectures that fit in with the choreographed curriculum. I lucked out. I had been giving the reproductive genetics lecture to the first-year medical students for the past five years.

I reviewed with them that chromosomes are our genetic material packaged in all the cells of our body. A man has forty-six chromosomes, including an X and a Y chromosome, written as 46XY. A normal woman has two X chromosomes (46XX). Therefore, a woman can only pass an X chromosome to her children, while a man can pass either an X or a Y chromosome to his children. When two X chromosomes are present, the offspring is known genetically as a female, whether or not the sex organs (ovaries and uterus) are present. When X and Y chromosomes are present, the offspring is a genetic male, whether or not the male sex organs (penis and testes) are present. However, disorders of sexual differentiation do occur—known as disorder of sexual differentiation or DSD. A 46XY DSD used to be called a male pseudohermaphrodite, a genetic male with disorders of testicular development and hormonal production. While a 46XX DSD used to be called a female pseudohermaphrodite, a genetic female with male hormone excess.

Bob's chromosome evaluation demonstrated 46XX, a genetic female. The CT scan demonstrated ovaries bilaterally together with a pair of fallopian tubes and a remnant uterus just behind what appeared to be a small but normal prostate gland. This was remarkable! Bob represented a unique patient—a true hermaphrodite with a complete set of both male and female organs.

True hermaphrodites most often have Bob's karyotype of 46XX. However, they only have female sex organs on one side and male sex organs on the other—not like Bob who has a paired set of both male and female organs. In these 46XX males, sperm production is usually nonexistent because the Y chromosome, which has the sperm-producing region on it, is absent. That's why the finding of any sperm production at all on Bob's biopsy was so exciting.

The Y chromosome is made up of two regions—one short and one long. The short region has the SRY gene—also called the testis determining factor. The long region of the Y chromosome has the genes that control sperm production. Bob's variation had the SRY gene, located on another chromosome. That would be the only way he would have testes. With this SRY gene being located on another chromosome that is not an X or Y chromosome, this inborn error can be passed down to his descendants. Something that Bob and Debra needed to know. That is, if we can have him make sperm. For that, we needed to activate the genes that control sperm production. He obviously had these genes since sperm production was noted on the testis biopsy. We just didn't know where they were located. At least not yet.

Bob was born with a penis, scrotum, and two testicles and therefore looked to the rest of the world like a male and had been reared as a male. It was probably the reason that the governor chose him to bring home from the hospital. It was rare for true hermaphrodites to have their ovaries past their teens since most had surgery to remove their abnormal gonads within the first few years of life. Bob was one of those rare individuals who was born with and still had intact ovaries *and* testes.

However, there was no question as to the appropriate medical treatment. Since Bob had the external male sex organs and had been reared as a male, the only appropriate course was removal of the tissue that would tend to feminize him and has suppressed his sperm production. The ovaries, fallopian tubes, and any remnant uterus that was present would also need to be removed. The removal of testicular tissue would only be indicated if a tumor was present, and if it were, removal of the entire testis would be the only appropriate course of action.

However, Dr. Brunswick hadn't sent the entire testis for testing, and the small fragment that was sent didn't indicate a tumor. Therefore, it was inexplicable why Dr. Brunswick stated he removed the testis yet didn't send it all for pathological evaluation. Not only would this be unethical, but it could also subject him to criminal investigation. My distrust in Dr. Brunswick grew. But he was not an incompetent physician. I knew there must have been an ulterior motive—one that made him willingly subject himself to the possible loss of his medical license and one he intended to personally benefit from.

I asked Bob and Debra to come to my office together at the end of my office hours to discuss treatment options. I purposely wanted it to be at the end of hours at my office. I needed to have the appropriate amount of time to discuss his evaluation and what it meant. There were sure to be a lot of questions—most of them difficult, if not impossible, to answer. However, I wanted to restore Bob's self-confidence as much as I could. I had a nagging feeling that I was missing something. A reason that could explain Dr. Brunswick's actions. Prior to our meeting today, I had arranged for both Bob and Debra to meet our team psychologist, Dr. Gregg Alport. I felt they would need his help afterward.

I spoke with Gregg prior to my meeting with Bob and Debra. He acknowledged the repressed hostility that Bob had toward Dr. Brunswick, and that this might cause resistance on Bob's part toward any treatment plans. The unemotional way Bob retold his interactions with Dr. Brunswick also piqued Gregg's curiosity. Instead of showing outward signs of anger and frustration with his treatment, he was unemotional, as if he were retelling someone else's story.

13

CONSULTATION

The evening of our meeting arrived. Bob walked in several steps behind Debra. His head was down, and he moved with an almost shuffling gait. Not like the "always in control" Bob I knew. As if he knew something was up and was anticipating bad news.

"Hi, Bob. Hi, Debra." I hoped to hide any hint of concern in my intonation.

"Hi, Dr. Gifford," Bob stated in an almost muffled and incomprehensible fashion. "Thank you for seeing us so late this evening." This was not like Bob.

"Bob, why so down in the dumps?" I asked.

"Problems at work, problems at home, and Dr. Brunswick's findings that there was no tumor in the testis biopsy."

"Well, that's great. Why so glum?"

"He also said that I didn't produce any sperm, and that I would never be able to have children of my own. I feel like a freak!" His eyes welled up with tears.

"Well, let's take a fresh look at all this. Isn't that why you're here?" I was acting as professionally as I could, knowing full well that our discussion tonight would make him feel even worse.

"I understand what you're saying. I just can't get this feeling out of me," Bob said.

"What do you mean? What kind of feeling?" I responded.

"It's a sensation of...emptiness," Bob said. "It makes me feel like I'm all alone. You know, like when you were a kid and something terrible suddenly happened, like having your best friend move away. You know it's bad, but you don't feel the pain right away. However, you feel as if your life just suddenly changed direction. You feel empty inside: no future, no present, just the past, as if everyone else went forward but you."

"It's funny. When you get older, you don't stop having those feelings, and you never get used to it." A brief pause followed. "I'm sorry for taking up your time with this, Doctor. What did you find?"

I always felt a little embarrassed when a patient called me doctor. Maybe it was the expectations that came along with the title—the expectations that all would be well. I always made it a point to introduce myself with my first and last name, thinking I was diffusing the patient's anxiety. I was trying in my own way to let the patient know that I'd do the best I could but that I was only human.

What Bob didn't know was that I had already seen Dr. Brunswick's workup. How was I to tell him about the female organs in his body? How was I to break the news to him that the surgery he had with Dr. Brunswick was, to say the least, inappropriate?

"Bob, it appears from the results of your evaluation with Dr. Brunswick that you have extra tissue in your body that might be releasing a hormone into your bloodstream. That hormone is preventing your testes from producing sperm." A brief pause followed.

"Do you mean I have a tumor?"

"No, you don't have cancer," I quickly responded. "As you might remember..."

And remember Bob did. He was a biology major in college and was accepted to several Ivy League medical schools, yet he decided not to attend. His heart was not in medicine.

In fact, he had a meltdown after college. For several years after college he had no direction. He bounced from job to job, usually staying no longer than a few weeks. He could well afford to do this; his family was one of the wealthiest in the state. One of the jobs he took was in the sporting goods section at Harley's, a large department store in town. That is when he met George. George was one of the other salesmen in sporting goods and had befriended Bob. George was a party animal, out late almost every night, oftentimes arriving to work with less than an hour or two of sleep but always meticulously dressed and groomed. Bob found out later that George was the son of the owner this very successful store. George loved being single, and the ladies loved him. He was almost the antithesis of Bob. Oh, for sure, Bob was always well dressed, but he was quite introverted. He found it difficult to strike up a conversation with women, and even with the guys, he would be quiet and pensive, almost as if he was removed from the conversation. Even though Bob worked for only a week at Harley's, they formed an enduring friendship.

It wasn't until his father took ill that he found his calling. He ran the family business in his father's absence and more than doubled its value in only a few years.

However, when he met Debra at a party at George's house, his life began anew. Debra was thirty at the time, and Bob was thirty-five.

14

FLASHBACK

It was three years after Debra had lost her husband, Tom, and their unborn child in that terrible automobile accident. She was working in an extremely high-pressure job as a VP in charge of compliance at a large securities firm, and she was very good at her job. This was her world. She had held this job for eight years before the accident. Now she would intentionally leave work late at night and travel home by train, possibly stopping by the corner food mart to pick up something to eat that evening. She would play her piano at night and sob endlessly. Her mourning was never ending.

She was so in love with her husband. They had planned and saved and talked about the future and had wanted so much to have children. It was this—their future together—that she missed. It was some time after the tragedy that she ran into George while shopping in Harley's. George was one of her husband's fraternity brothers during their college years. She had not seen much of him since her husband's death. In fact, she had not seen much of anyone. George had tried to keep in touch. She did not return his calls. It was on a rainy night that George called her, and she answered.

"Hey, Debra! Is that really you on the phone? I've been worried about you. Is everything all right?"

"George, I'm sorry I haven't gotten back to you."

"I've been missing you, Debra. Why haven't you returned my calls?"

"I'm really sorry. I just couldn't find much time recently with work and all." Debra still couldn't bear the prospect of stirring up old memories.

"Well, now that we've finally connected, how about coming by my place tonight? I'm having one of my good ol' TGIF parties."

"Thanks so much for asking, but…"

"Come on, Debra. We've been friends for a long time. You need to get out sometime."

Unbeknownst to her, George had asked Bob to help at the party and thought these two might hit it off.

Debra knew that George was right. It had been a long time. "I'll try to get there."

"I'm counting on you, Debra. See you at eight o'clock."

George's house was modeled after his frat house, Becus House, an old stately mansion. It was a Tudor in which time seemed to have stopped. The walls were solid plaster with real wooden lathe. The ceilings had sweeping arches with wooden beams and wrought iron casement windows. The floors were varnished oak. The only modern accents were recessed lights that were focused on beautiful original oil paintings of quaint European villages.

It was nearly 9:30 p.m. when Debra arrived. She almost didn't make it. It was raining, which made it difficult to get a cab. George was passing the front door when Debra arrived. He couldn't hold back his sheer joy when he saw her.

"I never thought you'd come," he said incredulously.

"Neither did I," she muttered.

"What did I do that made you come?"

"I guess it was what you said. That I needed to get out sometime. I really haven't, and I really needed to."

"Well, I'm glad you came. And feel free to help, as I know you will."

"Thanks, George," she said as she hugged him. "You're really a great friend."

George had asked Bob to make sure that the guests knew where to put their coats when they arrived. He would direct them to one of two massive closets that George had cleared out in advance of the party. Bob greeted a particularly beautiful woman immediately after George had greeted her. She had come to the party unescorted. Instead of showing her where to hang her coat, he helped her off with it and stated that he would hang it up in the first closet closest to the door. Her beauty and the kindness in her voice stunned him, and the simple action of her gracefully taking off her coat mesmerized him.

"Hi, I'm Bob, an old friend of George's. I'd really like to speak with you once all the guests arrive. Would you mind?" Pearls of moisture glistened on his brow as he pulled his collar to get a bit cooler.

Debra was equally smitten with her encounter. "That would be great. I really don't know anyone at this party besides George." As she walked away she looked back at Bob as he greeted the guests. He appeared to be enjoying his role as greeter. His smile was kind, his laugh engaging.

After the last rush of guests, Bob was finally free to join the party. He entered what George called the Grand Room. Most of the guests were congregating here. It was fifty feet long and forty feet wide with couches and chairs tastefully placed. Certainly not by George, Bob was thinking. Servers passed hors d'oeuvres, and two bartenders kept busy at a bar set up in the corner. Small beads of sweat were forming on Bob's forehead. He was not accustomed to not being in control of anything, let alone his emotions. He looked for Debra.

Debra was holding a champagne glass, walking through the hall, and admiring the architecture of George's eighteenth-century house. The smile on her face suggested a hint of loneliness. She recognized the party as reminiscent of the old fraternity days: drinking, carousing, and just plain old good times. *George was right,* she thought. *I needed this.* Debra didn't quite know what it was that attracted her to

Bob. It was possibly the crick in his lip caused by the impression of his pipe of years gone by, or maybe it was the dimple in his chin that would almost wink when he laughed. But it wasn't long after she arrived that they began talking. Bob started the conversation.

"Leave it up to George to find a place like this," Bob stated as he approached Debra from the side.

"He always was a man of impeccable taste," Debra replied. "Have you been here before?"

"Only when he first moved in a few months ago. I helped him move some furniture," George replied. "Have you?"

"No, I haven't. George has been asking me to come over, but I never seemed to find the time."

"Then what made you come tonight?"

"Something George said about needing to get out made sense." While looking and speaking with Bob, a smile was ever present on Debra's face. She was also laughing—laughing for the first time in three years.

Bob and Debra continued to talk throughout the evening and into morning. Bob escorted Debra home, and they made plans to see each other again the next day. Their relationship continued to blossom over the ensuing weeks, which turned into months. Debra once again was radiant with a smile that could light up a room. Curiously, the topic of children did not come up. Through George, Bob knew of Debra's horrific accident in which she lost her husband and unborn child and how devastated she had been afterward. He did not want those emotions to resurface. He was also conflicted about having children. He had a dysphoric feeling when he thought about having a family. He didn't know where it emanated from. It was one of the few things he could not control. They were married within the year.

15

ALL FOR SCIENCE

I continued my discussion with Bob and Debra. I brought out my favorite model to demonstrate. Interesting how you can break the tension in the air by using visuals. The model I use is a plastic relief of a cutaway of the male pelvis showing both the male genitalia and internal structures, including the prostate, bladder, and great vessels. Presenting a complex topic to patients with limited medical knowledge is always a challenge. A physician wants to make sure the patient understands but doesn't want to oversimplify. I found that using facial expressions and pausing for questions were the best way to make sure.

"Sperm are produced in the testes, and eggs are released from the ovaries. However, in addition to these gametes, hormones are also produced in these organs. Hormones are chemicals made by the body to provide communication between various organs. The testes produce testosterone, the primary male hormone responsible for your low voice, muscle and bone growth, and developing sperm. In your situation, Bob, extra tissue in your body is releasing an unusual hormone that is preventing your testes from producing sperm."

Bob was shifting uncomfortably in his chair. "What do you mean by unusual? Can we get rid of this tissue? Would doing it make me able to produce sperm?"

"I really think we can, Bob; however, I have to tell you something else that might not sit well with you." I felt a lump welling up in my throat.

"What's that?" he said with obvious concern.

"Bob, you might remember from your genetics classes that genetic sex is determined by the presence of a pair of special chromosomes called sex chromosomes. These are the X and Y chromosomes. A genetic male has both an X and a Y sex chromosome, while a genetic female has two X chromosomes."

"Yeah, I remember that."

"In addition," I continued, "the male has a sex-determining region on the Y chromosome called the SRY region that determines whether male hormones and the testes will develop. Occasionally, this region becomes attached to the X chromosome or any of the other twenty-two paired chromosomes instead of the Y chromosome."

I kept glancing at Debra as I was talking. I wanted to make sure that she not only understood but was not stunned by what I was saying.

"You were born with an XX pattern with the SRY region on one of your other chromosomes." I stopped and waited for Bob's response.

"What does that mean? Are you saying that I'm a female?"

"No, you're very much a man. However, you do have female chromosomes and some female tissue as a result."

"How much female tissue?"

This, I knew, was to be the most difficult part. "Well, it appears from the studies that have been completed that you have a complete set of female internal organs, including a uterus, two ovaries, and fallopian tubes that are connected to your male genital system at the level of the prostate." I put up the CT scan results and showed them the structures I was referring to.

Bob appeared nonplussed. A brief period of silence ensued.

Debra was great. She could have reacted with histrionics or an incredulous gasp, but she didn't. I knew at that time their relationship would survive, even though I suspected Bob was less than convinced.

"So, Bob," Debra said with a clearly upbeat tone, "you didn't even need me. You could have had a child by yourself!"

Even Bob chuckled at that.

We spent another hour that evening discussing how these anomalies developed. However, as the discussion progressed, Bob sat upright in the chair, his face reddened, and the dimple on his chin flattened.

"You mean I didn't need to have my testis removed?" he asked with evident irritation.

"Bob, if indeed you had a tumor, of course you should have had it removed." I tried to be as diplomatic as I could, but I knew Bob sensed my own anger at Dr. Brunswick's callous nature and inappropriate surgery. "However, I have found no evidence from your prior evaluation or the pathology that a tumor was present."

"Then why did he do it?" Bob inquired with anger. He was angrier at himself for being so naive to think that Brunswick, his biological brother, would have his best interests at heart. He probably should have been more mindful of Kevin's concern.

"I don't know. He might have a very good reason. I would certainly ask him."

"I certainly will. That bastard lied to me. So where do we go from here?"

"The approach is fairly standard. We remove all female organs, while of course protecting your remaining testis, vas deferens, and prostate."

"Is this a dangerous operation?"

"Bob, you're young and will do quite well. However, as you know, no procedure is without risk. One of the major risks, as I see it, is possible damage to your remaining testis or the tubes that take the sperm out of the testis. This would have a deleterious but treatable effect on your future fertility. There is also the possibility for major bleeding since the organs that need to be removed are near large blood vessels. I will, of course, take all precautions to prevent either of these complications from occurring."

"With these possibilities, do we need to do an operation? What if we left all as is?" Bob asked.

This was the Bob I knew: inquisitive and thoughtful. I answered his questions as best as I could. "Yes, you can. However, there is a risk of cancer developing in these organs that you do not need. Also, since the ovary and uterus are not easily felt on exam, it is difficult to follow them by physical examination alone. Imaging can be done along with measuring several blood markers for tumor; however, many in my field would recommend removal."

"But I'm not producing any sperm, am I?"

"Well, here's the good news. Although no sperm were seen in your ejaculate, your biopsy report indicated the potential for sperm. You have immature sperm cells that may not be mature enough or of sufficient quantity to be effective in fertilizing Debra's eggs, at least not in the standard fashion. However, the report also suggests that your sperm is being prevented from fully maturing. I reviewed the slides myself. Your sperm isn't developing into the tadpole-like cells we call spermatozoa. This finding is called maturation arrest and can be due to a hormone preventing the full maturation of sperm."

I could see a great sense of relief on both their faces upon hearing this, but Debra was almost aglow. "There is, in fact, some speculation in the medical journals," I continued, "that the female tissue present in your body is secreting a hormone that is suppressing both sperm and testosterone production in your testis. We just don't know what this substance is or what organ is producing it. If you decide to have the surgery I have suggested, I wanted to ask that you be part of our research so that we might isolate this substance."

"What type of research?"

I was glad Bob was asking questions. I wanted him to fully understand what we were about to discuss, particularly given the significant risks involved. "Bob, yours is a very rare case. Not only do you have a complete set of ovaries and testes, but your testes have germ cells—cells that can produce sperm. This is almost unheard of! I have reviewed the slides from your biopsy. In your case, they are not completing the maturation process into sperm capable of fertilizing an egg from Debra. I believe, as suggested from prior research studies, that a substance secreted from your ovaries, likely a hormone, is preventing your testis from producing mature sperm. The only problem is not knowing what this substance is. However, if I'm right, sperm production could increase in three to six months after removal of the ovaries."

"And if you're wrong?" Bob asked with concern.

"If I'm wrong, the sperm won't be produced, and the production that is already occurring in your remaining testis can be lost too. You might lose testosterone as well. To begin, I'll need to give you some hormones before and after the surgery to jump-start sperm production. We can also take a biopsy of your remaining testis to see what it's producing, and sperm bank any sperm that are present in the testicular tissue."

Bob's gaze drifted as he pondered what I had just said. He then looked at me and asked, "Is the biopsy and taking these hormones dangerous?"

"Well, unfortunately, there is some risk. As we discussed, the biopsy can cause damage to your testis. This is unlikely but possible. The purpose of taking a small piece for banking is to make sure that we preserve the fertility you presently have—no matter what. The hormones we want to stimulate are normally produced in an area of the brain called the pituitary. Let me explain, and please stop me if you have any questions."

I took out a note pad and drew the structures involved in the hormonal control of sperm and testosterone production as I was talking to Bob and Debra. I pointed to the pituitary gland. "It's here in the pituitary that a multitude of hormones are released and travel to specific organs, like the testes, and control their functions. The two hormones of primary interest are called FSH and LH in men and are also known as follicle stimulating hormone and luteinizing hormone in women. These hormones are responsible for the production of testosterone. LH and FSH work in concert to ensure maturation of the sperm along the wall of the seminiferous tubules in the testes. In women, these same hormones stimulate the ovaries to further mature the oocytes, or eggs, that are there. I believe that you are producing two types of FSH: one that directly stimulates the ovaries, and one that directly stimulates the testes." I labeled FSHo and FSHt on my diagram.

I continued, "The problem with giving you these hormones is that the one that stimulates the ovaries will cause the ovaries to mature many eggs at once. These changes are often painful. In addition, the maturation of the eggs occurs with growth of the follicles that contain the egg surrounded by a cystic cavity. Many cells in the follicle can and do produce hormones. However, excessive hormone production can cause very serious side effects, including increasing the leakiness of small vessels that might result in accumulation of fluid in your abdomen, around your lungs, or even around your heart. This could lower your blood pressure and even cause death. Long term, these hormones could damage vital organs such as your kidneys. In addition, if indeed your ovaries are producing a substance that suppresses sperm production, and we stimulate it to produce a high level of these hormones, it might not be able to be reversed. You might never produce sperm. There is also some data in the literature that these hormones might cause cancer years later."

"It sure seems like a lot of downside. Would you agree to it?" Bob asked with trepidation.

"I guess not, Bob. Except for..."

"Except for what?" Bob asked.

"Well, I doubt that your remaining testicular tissue will ever produce mature sperm that can be used to fertilize Debra's egg without giving you hormones to stimulate it. However, if we gave you these hormones, which we call gonadotropins because they work on the gonads, we would also increase the substance that I believe is suppressing your sperm production. What I propose to do is to selectively shut down the part of your pituitary that is secreting the FSHt and then use FSHo to hyperstimulate your ovaries and hopefully produce and secrete this unknown substance. My goal would be to isolate it from your blood and be able to reconstruct it in the laboratory. We would then proceed to remove your female organs and restart sperm production with hormonal stimulation using FSHt."

Bob moved forward in his chair, and his face lit up. "Can this really be done?"

"I believe it can based on some recent work from a noted Belgian researcher. However, there are drawbacks to this approach, not the least of which is that we have no knowledge of what other effects this unknown hormone has and whether its production would have undesirable side effects. In addition, the hormones used to stop pituitary function might also suppress the entire pituitary gland, which controls not only the ovaries and testes but also the thyroid and adrenal gland. However, I don't believe that this is likely since the FSHt is specific for the testes. We would only then need to give you a pill to block the excess estrogen released by the ovaries. When the testis is completely suppressed, and the estrogen produced from the ovary is blocked, there will be no inhibition of pituitary function, and therefore pituitary secretion would be maximal. I would then remove the ovaries and stop FSHt suppression. The hope then would be that the now stimulated pituitary would result in rebound sperm production. There is also a bright side to this—even if it is remote."

"What's that?" Bob inquired.

"There is a very real possibility that the substance we recover might have significant medical use." I knew Bob would need to know that there might be significant commercial application.

"Do you mean that there's a possibility that my body produces a substance that could help others?"

I felt that Bob was looking for some meaning in all that was happening to him—some way of turning his despair into something positive. "Even bigger than that. It could result in the first male contraceptive pill. It would be as significant a finding as the discovery of penicillin."

Bob sat back again in his chair, his brows furrowed, his lips pursed. "Isn't there danger in that?"

"In what way?" I didn't know what he meant. However, the question intrigued me, and so did his answer.

"Well, if this is potentially so big, aren't there others who would stop at nothing to get it?" Bob questioned, almost as if he were asking himself the question. This singular question seemed to be a turning point in Bob's demeanor. He began to take charge of his destiny. Although we didn't know it at the time, this was also the beginning of a harrowing ordeal for both of us.

Bob was certainly his father's son—always the businessman, always with forethought. He could emotionally separate himself from any situation when it came to business. He certainly was right. It had already crossed my mind. If we were to proceed, we would have to protect our work, and since Bob was the host, we should protect Bob.

"I suppose you have a point there. It's certainly not my area of expertise. How would you suggest we proceed?" I asked, knowing that Bob would have a logical approach.

"Well, as I see it, I don't have many choices. I either take the hormonal stimulation prior to and possibly after surgery and at least have a chance of producing sperm, or I just go through the operation to remove the organs I don't need, and we either adopt a child or Debra undergoes artificial insemination with someone else's sperm."

"That's essentially right, although we could try to extract the immature sperm from the testis and inject it into an egg removed from Debra. However, the probability of success in your case is not very high."

"Then that settles it!" Bob responded emphatically. "We proceed as you have suggested, with one addition: I'll have my attorney draw up an agreement between us that gives you exclusive rights to pursue your research and gives us joint rights to use any substance resulting from this work for commercial purposes. The one problem I see is that we will quickly have to patent any product found to claim it as ours."

I was amazed at this response—and quite embarrassed. Although I thought about the commercial potential, his direct approach made it seem as if this was my intent from the start.

"Bob, the likelihood of reaping financial reward is remote, and even if that is possible, I never intended to profit from it. Any agreement should give you, and you alone, any financial windfall."

"With all due respect, that's the problem with you doctors, at least the honest ones like yourself. You never look ahead. The larger picture is lost in your monocular view of the world. Maybe that's why the medical profession is in the situation it is with managed care—accepting whatever is offered for fear of loss of income and without any thought of the long-term ramifications. Just no business sense. No, Dr. Gifford, we're in this together. I know that it's best for me if you have a vested interest in all this. Besides, you're doing all the work. I'm just the lab rat!"

"We can certainly discuss this further later. Give it some more thought. After you've had time to think about all we've gone over this evening, get back to me."

16

INSIDE MAN

Bob continued to meet with Kevin at the diner. Some of the time, they continued to catch up on the years they were separated. Kevin particularly wanted to know about their dad. Bob would relay stories about growing up. The many times that their dad was away and the cadre of caretakers. He spoke about his stepmother, stepbrother and stepsister. Kevin spoke about his loving parents and his wife, Beth. The love of his life. They had decided that at least for now they would not tell their families about each other. Not knowing how emotionally stable Brunswick was, they did not want to place their families in jeopardy. Their conversations always circled back to Brunswick.

"Bob, we need to keep tabs on Brunswick. Something screwy about that guy. He may be our brother, but I don't think he's normal. Look, he didn't do right by you, and I know you're not a fan, but it really needs to be you," Kevin said.

"I don't disagree. Just concerned about our families if he finds out. Debra is already scared of him," Bob replied.

"I know, I know. But what is that expression—better to keep your friends close and your enemies closer,". Kevin said.

"I received a call from his office last week. The secretary said Brunswick was looking for investors in his business and thought I might want a tour of ReproMed. I was noncommittal. Don't really like the guy, and not sure what other motive he might have for getting me there. What do you think?" Bob asked Kevin.

"Well, from what I found out," Kevin began, "ReproMed is a genetic testing and research facility. It is also a very profitable business. The business recently took a large loan from a bank. I know this because one of my guys heads up money laundering for the department. The banks are required to report sizable loans to us. The size of his loan must have been very large since the bank reported it to his group. We were talking, and I asked him if he knew of this company. Told him I was thinking of getting tested and wanted to know if it was a reputable place to go. He kidded me about having to get tested to see if I was the father of an illegitimate child."

"What did you tell him?" Bob asked.

"I just let him know that there was a family disease that all members of the family were getting tested for. That seemed to quiet him. He told me he had no bad news about ReproMed. He thought it was just another company getting over its head in debt," Kevin replied.

"Good," Bob said. "Don't feel it is the right time to let others know about this. Not until we know what he is up to."

"Exactly," Kevin said. "That is the reason you should go for the tour. See what is going on at ReproMed.

Bob called and set up the tour. ReproMed was located five blocks from MUH. It occupied two floors in a twenty-five-story building with a front glass facade that reflected the morning light. It had an underground parking lot. The administrative offices were on the tenth floor; the laboratories were one floor below. Bob was impressed by the size of the enterprise. He was also impressed by the number of security guards employed.

He was escorted to Brunswick's office by one of the larger security guards. They were all dressed in blue sport jackets and ties with khaki-colored slacks. A ReproMed emblem adorned each guard's sport jacket pocket. A bulge was present underneath the coat. These guards were also well armed.

Brunswick greeted Bob with a smile, which was unusual for him, and a firm handshake. "Glad you could make it," he said. "I am very proud of what we built. Let me show you around."

Brunswick proceeded to spend the next hour taking Bob around the administrative offices on the tenth floor. He met several of the principals in the company who were eager to discuss the financial statements and business projections. Very little time was spent on the projects under development. In fact, the tour of the ninth-floor laboratories lasted less than five minutes. Bob made note of the locked rooms on the ninth floor with large red signs labeled No Entry. When he inquired what these rooms were, he was told that they had either dangerous reagents or sensitive patient records.

At the end of the tour, Brunswick took Bob back to his office. Bob thought he knew what was coming. A pitch to become an investor. He was not prepared for what Brunswick was about to tell him.

"Bob, I asked you here to show you what I have built but also to tell you something. Something I have known for a while. Your genetic tests show that we are related. In fact, we are brothers, born the same day. Our mother died during childbirth. I suspect during your birth," Brunswick added, knowing the effect it would have on Bob. He knew how to push buttons.

"You're kidding me!" Bob said, trying to be as surprised as possible about this revelation he already knew about.

"No, I am not. Genetic testing does not lie," Brunswick said.

"What genetic testing?" Bob inquired. He had only consented to the sibling genetic testing with Kevin. *Did he know about Kevin?*

"We have a large database at ReproMed. I found you had testing performed and took the liberty of confirming it with blood testing and tissue testing during your surgery," Brunswick calmly replied. "And I need your help."

"Need my help?" Bob emphasized the word *help*. "You may be my genetic sibling, but you did not have my permission to take samples from me. Why didn't you just ask me?"

Brunswick's demeanor suddenly changed. The smile left his face. A scowl was apparent. He made no apologies. Only a threat. "Listen, Bob, I know you have developed a respect for Dr. Gifford, and I am sure he feels the same about you. That is why you are going to be my inside man. I want you to let me know what he is doing and what he has found out. You do this for me, and I will make sure no harm comes to Debra." Brunswick was eerily calm as he said this.

Bob was now convinced this man, his biological brother, was seriously psychotic. He wasn't sure how to respond, but he needed to know what he knew. "Why the focus on Dr. Gifford? There must be other researchers who are doing similar work," he said.

"Not my work!" Brunswick stated possessively. "He also may be our third brother. I have a partial match from his employment blood testing at the hospital. Need to get some additional testing to be sure."

Bob was unnerved. He could not believe how this information was able to get into Brunswick's hands. *Is there no privacy?* he wondered. He was at least relieved that Kevin was not under suspicion. He was also convinced he needed to play along. He couldn't place Debra in danger. He also felt he had to protect Barry Gifford. He needed Kevin's help.

He agreed to meet with Brunswick weekly to update him. He had no choice. Brunswick set up an office on the tenth floor of ReproMed for Bob to use when he visited. Bob also met with Kevin. He updated Kevin on his visit with Brunswick. Kevin started keeping an eye on Barry Gifford.

17

REALIZATION

Bob didn't take very long to get back to me. The next morning, he called me on my cell, confirming his decision. Curiously, the caller ID showed ReproMed's number, not Bob's. I had no idea why that was, but I made a mental note to ask him about it. He also wanted to let me know that his attorney, Charles Walsh, would be calling me to discuss my thoughts on patenting, especially considering my connection with the university.

We had scheduled surgery to remove Bob's female organs (his ovaries, fallopian tubes, and uterus). I called Bob and asked him to come by the office later in the week to discuss the protocol. I was concerned as to how Bob would handle the hormonal treatment and surgery and thought it best to have him consult again with Gregg Alport. Bob agreed.

I met with Bob's attorney, who preferred to be called Charles. He was a University of Pennsylvania graduate with an uncanny ability to get to the meat of the situation almost immediately. He and Bob were made for each other. Both were decisive, and both were Yankees fans. In fact, it was at a Yankees game that they wound up sitting next to each other and commiserating over a recent trade for a pitcher from Texas for another well-liked Yankee pitcher who had become involved with a teammate's wife. Reminiscent of the Fritz-Peterson scandal and subsequent trade. They never knew quite why this drew them together, but it had resulted in a very profitable relationship for both.

We also began the patent application for the substance we anticipated we would find after Bob's surgery. It was a bit presumptuous but necessary given the potential value of a discovery of this magnitude. There was always a concern with a procedure like this that required much operative time and many assistants—could we really keep it secret? And what if someone got wind of our results and published them first? A patent was a good idea.

There were many concerns I had regarding Bob's ability to cope with what he was about to undergo. Hell, anyone in the same situation would. Not only the physical but also the emotional turmoil that always accompanied the realization that one's body was not perfect, that nature had played a cruel trick. That's why I asked Gregg to talk with Bob during the weeks prior to surgery. Gregg had a lot of experience with patients like Bob. It was not only his training that made him so special but also his life experience. His brother had had cancer when he was young and now had much difficulty conceiving. His compassion and perseverance to find the right place for his brother and sister-in-law to undergo in vitro fertilization is what kept his brother's marriage together.

Bob and Gregg met several times prior to surgery. Each time they met, they discussed Bob's life. Bob grew up in a dysfunctional family. He was the oldest of three children. His mother had died at childbirth, and his father remarried shortly afterward. His father and stepmother had two children. His parents had their favorite. That was his youngest sister, Lynn. Unfortunately, little did they know that their pride and joy was no angel. In high school, she would steal away from home in the evenings for a tryst with several different teachers over the years. She was indeed brilliant but also had a bit of help along the way. His younger brother, Jack, was the smartest of them all yet had no direction. He secured his father's approval by excelling at Harvard, which allowed him to continue his income from the family business while continuing to lead the life of a playboy.

Bob was the serious one. He was always concerned about the future, especially the direction the family's business would take. Ludlow Enterprises was a multinational electronics firm with interests in many diverse areas from telecommunications to biocircuits. It was Bob, however, who single-handedly took the firm public after his father's illness and untimely death, making millionaires of all who invested and billionaires of his immediate family.

However, it was Bob's ability to motivate that made him special, and this trait was the reason for his success. He could be so effective because he listened. He would come into a meeting and just sit and listen. Without saying a word, he would understand the issues and develop a plan. He was a master of organizing the troops, and in making them proud to be part of the plan. He was also able to separate his emotional self from his intellectual and inquisitive self. He could implement what was right and not necessarily popular. He was respected for this. However, it wasn't always this way. Bob went through a period when he didn't know exactly what he wanted from life. He couldn't adjust. Sure, he came from a privileged existence, but that didn't instill self-confidence. He was quite uncoordinated when he was young. He never could hit in stickball, so he stopped trying. He also had those ears that would always stick out from the side of his hat. His crew cut certainly didn't help. His folks had wanted him to go to medical school. A "respectable profession," as they said. But Bob wanted something more than studying and regurgitating facts that were "drilled into you by a professor who last saw a patient twenty years prior!" he would quip. For sure, he was smart—smart as a whip—and that was what finally made him find his direction. He was smart enough to know that his happiness was more important to him than his parents' expectations of him. The discussion with his folks wasn't easy. More than once, tempers flared, yet in the end, he made it known that this was the way it would be.

18

SURGERY

Wednesday, August 5, 1992

It was raining on the day Bob's surgery was scheduled at MUH. It usually slowed me down. I found it very relaxing when it was raining. Possibly that was why my colleagues were so productive in Seattle. I was told it rains almost 50 percent of the time there. It could be that gray skies activated the pineal gland, and the increase in melatonin caused the calming effect. This day was different. I was up early. This was not the day to be relaxed. I needed to be at the top of my game today. I couldn't let the rain blunt the edge I needed. Bob's future, and possibly his life, depended on me.

I got up early to meet the team at the hospital and set up for the surgical procedure. There were usually five members of the surgical team: the operating surgeon and first assistant, an anesthesiologist, a scrub nurse, and a circulating nurse. We had a few additional team members today.

The anesthesiologist stayed at the head of the operating room table during the procedure, making sure the blood pressure and pulse stayed within limits while carefully adjusting the anesthetic gases. Although anesthesiologists wore scrubs, they did not wear sterile gowns or sterile gloves and were not trained to take part in the actual surgery. Dr. David Anderson was assigned to Bob's procedure. I was very fortunate. After twenty years in the anesthesiology department, he was the go-to person. When his colleagues had a particularly difficult intubation, an intraoperative cardiac emergency, or an unstable patient, they would always want Dr. Anderson nearby. Maybe his assignment should have alerted me. It should have, but it didn't.

The two nurses assigned to the room usually covered all cases that the room had for the day. Today we had Nona as the scrub nurse, and Ed as the circulator. I didn't know Ed. He was new. But Nona and I went way back. When I was just out of my residency and starting at Metropolitan University Hospital, she took me under her wing. I was scared of her at first. She had no qualms about berating any physician she felt was incompetent or egocentric. I certainly didn't want to be on her blacklist. She was also the best scrub nurse in the hospital. That's why when anyone tried to complain about her insolence, no one listened. When she was the scrub nurse, surgery became a carefully choreographed dance.

Ed was the circulating nurse and was the unknown. He was about six foot three with a dark complexion and long coarse hair that was pulled back into a disheveled ponytail. His hands were large with a leathery texture. However, it was his bloodshot eyes that were unsettling. His eyelids slightly closed with his eyes darting eerily from side to side. The circulating nurse brought supplies into the room that might be needed and replenished the surgical table with sterile supplies—an essential function but not usually vital, unless things go wrong. As every surgeon had heard many times, "If you don't have complications, you aren't operating enough." I always thought this statement was made to console those unfortunate souls who had things go wrong in the operating room, not because of an error on their part but because of factors they had no control over. I never wanted to invoke this statement and certainly not on this day.

Two surgical residents, Dr. Miguel Sanchez and Dr. Robert Munkowsky, were also assisting. In a teaching hospital such as MUH, residents were always scrubbed in on the cases. It was up to the attending surgeon—the surgeon the patient gave consent to—to decide just how much to allow the resident, or in this case residents, to do during the case. Although these residents were excited to be in on this case, they probably knew that they would get to do very little.

There is always a lot of preparation prior to a once-in-a-lifetime case like this. I needed to run the operation through my mind several times. I also hit the books to review all possible contingencies—the "what ifs" that always seemed to crop up. Sure, you can't anticipate all of them, but it makes you feel confident when you walk into the operating room. It was very much like studying for those standardized tests in high school. You could never really study as much as you would like to. You did your best by reviewing as many exams as you could beforehand. This made the tests a little less intimidating and certainly more doable. In fact, med school was really very similar.

It's a special privilege being a surgeon—operating on a patient with whom you have more than a doctor-physician relationship. Bob and I weren't close friends. That would make it almost impossible to be emotionally detached, as I must be to make those difficult decisions that would always be required in surgeries like his, decisions that will affect the rest of his life. I had many sleepless nights anticipating every possible complication that could arise.

I had taken myself through the procedure many times. The approach would be through a vertical incision just below the umbilicus, known as the belly button, and extending to the pubic symphysis, the bony prominence superior to the penis. This would allow full pelvic exposure while ensuring that he would have minimal scarring. I could always extend it above the umbilicus if necessary. I had discussed with Bob the possibility of using a more minimally invasive technique of laparoscopy or a robotic approach. However, I felt that the anatomy was not standard, bleeding was inevitable, and the best way to control it would be through a primary open approach. Bob agreed. I couldn't anticipate how important this decision would be.

I would proceed to the ovaries, first identifying and ligating the ovarian and uterine arteries, which would effectively isolate these organs and cut off their blood supply. This would lead to the most difficult and potentially dangerous part of the operation: removing his uterus. The major problem was its location. The CT images had localized it between the bladder and rectum, which is standard. However, it should also be attached to his prostate, which is not that bad, except for the fact that we wanted to retain his sexual function. The nerves and blood vessels responsible for erection were most likely adherent to the uterus, not to mention the major venous drainage from the prostate was nearby. I had to be careful with the vascular supply. I had no way of knowing where the blood supply would be derived from or drain to. There were bound to be a few anomalies present. It would be a little like walking into a minefield blindfolded.

There were twelve operating rooms in the main building at MUH and six additional in the ambulatory surgery center located a half mile from the main hospital. We were scheduled to be in room five, a large room with an operating microscope permanently mounted to the ceiling that made using it as simple as covering it with a sterile drape and lowering it to the surgical field.

Walking into the white operating amphitheater—white ceiling, off-white walls, and white-speckled floor—imbued one with emotion. For the patient, this could be fear. For the nurses, this could mean complacency with the routine of an emotionally charged environment. The room was environmentally controlled and kept at a cool sixty-eight degrees Fahrenheit. This was a great temperature for the surgeons who were gowned in a fluid-impervious material that does not allow body heat to readily escape. The gown, together with the surgical hat and mask, were confining, some might say claustrophobic. Many medical students had quickly chosen other medical specialties when subjected to the self-imposed imprisonment of being scrubbed into a long case and not able to even take a bathroom break while enduring the restrictive movements required to maintain sterility within the operating room.

Room five was recently upgraded with a new set of overhead lights that were easily positioned to focus light on the operative area. Bob arrived in the operating room with the circulating nurse who had confirmed his identity in the holding area and walked him down the hallway. His IV had already been started, and the nurse was holding the bag at the level of Bob's heart so that the fluid would drip into him.

As Bob entered the room, he was loquacious and probably a bit nervous. "I hope everyone had a good night's sleep. I wouldn't want any sex change procedures!"

After the routine introductions of the patient and the team, the patient was asked to lie down on the narrow operating room table by the circulating nurse.

I approached Bob's right side. "We'll take great care of you." I looked directly into his eyes.

"Any way I can help?" Bob queried with a twinkle in his eye.

"As you drift off to sleep, just dream of sperm jumping over a fence," I suggested. This imagery, changed from counting sheep jumping over a fence, always returned a laugh from the patient and chuckles from the operating room staff. It was also an attempt to lower the tension in the room.

Bob's arms were positioned on arm boards perpendicular to his sides. Variable compression stockings were placed on his legs to assure continued circulation and reduce the incidence of clots forming in his legs while he was asleep. A baseline blood pressure, ventilation gases, and a cardiac rhythm were analyzed. Dr. Anderson began preparing the patient. He gave him medications to make him relax and ultimately sleep. Bob was intubated without difficulty.

"All yours!" Dr. Anderson exclaimed when he was satisfied that Bob was properly induced and ready for the procedure. Ed entered 7:48 a.m. into the computer as the release time.

Dr. Munkowsky took the cue and began shaving Bob's hair that would be in the operative field, and he scrubbed and prepped the area for surgery. Bob was then draped with sterile surgical drapes, and the standard time-out was done. A surgical time-out is like a pilot's checklist before, during, and after a flight to verify that all functions of the airplane and necessary data are present and correct. Interestingly, all regulatory authorities had recently required the time-out in response to a plethora of wrong-site surgery. In the surgical time-out, participants in the surgical procedure introduced themselves to the patient, and they all stated and confirmed what surgery is to be done. All relevant imaging, supplies, and possible implants were reviewed and confirmed to be present.

Dr. Sanchez, as senior resident, was first assisting and stood directly across the table from me. He was a fifth-year surgical resident rotating on urology and a truly superb surgical resident. I was very fortunate to have him first assisting today. Next to him was Nona, the scrub nurse, and next to me was Dr. Munkowsky, the second assist. The procedure began with the low vertical incision through the skin. The rectus muscles were separated, and the anatomy was visualized.

We were all in awe of the way nature can sometimes create an abnormality. It was a remarkable site! We were able to clearly visualize the aberrant anatomy. The ovaries and uterus were pristine and exactly where they should be in a woman. The cervix of the uterus was adherent to the prostate, as expected. However, dense fibrous tissue appeared to be surrounding this area. I anticipated that this was going to be a difficult dissection since the blood vessels to the uterus were embedded in this dense tissue. I had no way of knowing where the larger arteries and veins supplying this region were in relation to this scar tissue. However, isolating and removing the ovaries and fallopian tubes were textbook. We proceeded quickly through this part.

All was going well until we started to isolate the uterine veins. As anticipated, they were stuck in the fibrous scar-like tissue. They also seemed a bit larger than usual and very adherent to the pelvic sidewall. I had Dr. Sanchez hold the retractors, while I attempted to free these vessels in preparation to tie them off.

"Dr. Gifford," Dr. Sanchez exclaimed with obvious distress. "Blood is welling up everywhere. Do you want me to move the retractors?"

"No, Miguel, you're doing great." I dared not have him move for fear of losing control of the bleeding. At a time like this, you don't think—you react. "Laps," I ordered as I began placing each lap pad purposely in the pelvis to contain the blood. "Sucker." I used the sucker to suction up the rising pool of blood and carefully moved each lap pad just slightly to hopefully identify the source of bleeding. The lap pad often tamponades the bleeding. Removing the lap pad or moving it too quickly might cause further bleeding or tearing of other vessels.

I didn't realize we were losing so much blood until Dr. Anderson asked, "Hey, Barry, whatcha doing down there? His blood pressure is dropping and becoming difficult to control with fluids."

"Got a bleeder here in the pelvis. I think it's a big one. Better send for blood."

It must have been only seconds later that all hell broke loose.

"Barry, I can barely get a pressure," Dr. Anderson said. "I've already given three liters of fluids, and the pulse rate is slowing."

"Did you push pressors yet?" I forced myself to maintain my composure as I continued my frantic search for the source of the bleeding.

"It's in the line now."

"We need central access to give fluids, fast." I knew it wouldn't be long before his heart gave out—either an ischemic event or an arrhythmia that would be fatal. "Dr. Munkowsky," I said to my second assist, "break scrub and help Dr. Anderson with a central line. Nona will help me here." It would be five minutes at least before another anesthesiologist would be here to help. Five minutes could make the difference between life and death. It was much more important to help stabilize Bob at this point. With Dr. Sanchez, Dr. Munkowsky, and Nona assisting me, I had enough hands in the field already.

I felt my heart ready to explode as I began wondering how I got myself into this situation. I also was determined that Bob was not going to die. The blood arrived just as the central line was in.

"I found the hole!" I exclaimed with relief. It was an aberrant vessel that must have torn from its insertion into the external iliac vein. "Hand me the Statinsky! Six-oh proline on a vascular needle! Sponge, sucker."

"Pressure is starting to return," Dr. Anderson called out with obvious relief.

"I have control," I responded. I was so glad we had decided to do this case as an open case and not use the laparoscope. Bob would have died in the time it took to open and gain control.

"Blood pressure one ten over sixty. Keeping me on my toes, eh, Barry," Dr. Anderson stated with his customary smirk.

"That wasn't fun." I started to regain my composure.

Bob was in the hospital for several days after his surgery. Kevin was a frequent visitor while Bob was recuperating. He made sure that it was at times Debra wasn't there. They spoke about their families, however, they never arranged to get their families together or even discuss their relationship. They felt this was best, given Brunswick's mental instability. They needed to know what Brunswick's plan was.

Dexter Brunswick stopped by to visit Bob on his post-op day three. Fortunately, they heard him talking to the nurse in the hallway. Kevin made a quick exit. Bob wondered what Brunswick was up to. Could not be good. Brunswick entered his room.

"Bob, how are you feeling?" Brunswick asked as if they were old friends.

"Fine, Dr. Brunswick. Very nice of you to stop by. How did you know I was here?" Bob inquired.

"I keep track of all my friends—and family," he said with a grin. "Heard you had quite an operation. Lost a good deal of blood. How are you feeling?" he inquired.

"Not bad, considering," Bob replied.

"Well, that's good. Wanted to make sure that you remembered our agreement. I'll see you next week." Brunswick left as quickly as he had appeared.

Bob knew what Dexter Brunswick wanted. He also knew what Brunswick would do if he obtained the information he sought. He had to stop him. He had to protect Debra too.

19

TESBLOC

Although he lost eight units of blood during surgery, Bob bounced back as if it were only a minor procedure. He maintained the determination to not only survive but to conquer. I really believed that his goal to be a father and the love of his wife brought him through the surgery and allowed his rapid recovery.

Bob became more than a patient and a partner. He became a friend and an impassioned supporter. He expended great time and effort on this project. He was driven. Without him, I'm not sure we would have come so far.

As we planned, we had collected blood specimens to analyze by stimulating Bob with FSHo prior to surgery. These specimens were then cryopreserved. About four months after surgery, I had Bob back in. It was time to start stimulating his testis with gonadotropins.

"Bob, how are you feeling?" I asked.

"Great!" he answered with his usual upbeat persona.

"It is time to start stimulating your testis with hormones, so they can produce testosterone and sperm. Your most recent blood tests showed your testosterone is low, so that is our first job. We will be starting you on an injectable medication called human chorionic gonadotropin. You probably have heard it called HCG. This is similar to LH, the hormone your pituitary makes to stimulate the cells in your testis to produce testosterone. Once your testosterone is in the normal range, we will add the drug we spoke about before, FSHt, to hopefully stimulate your testes to produce sperm. Do you have questions before I show you how to inject the medication?" I asked.

"No, Doc. I am ready. How long before we know if it works?" Bob inquired.

"Usually testosterone will increase within a month," I explained. "But we will wait at least another month before starting you on the FSHt. It will then be another three to six months on both these medications before we check to see if you have sperm in your ejaculate. If we do, we will freeze the sperm for use in an IVF procedure with your wife."

Bob seemed to understand completely.

"I'll show you how to inject, but before you start the medications, let's get a semen analysis to check if we have any sperm present now."

"Is that possible?" Bob asked.

"Well, if our theory is correct, the ovaries we removed would have been producing a substance that would have inhibited sperm production from your testis. Given the months since your surgery, it is possible. However, I believe you will likely still need to take these medications to maximize your production."

Bob was all in. He could not wait to get started.

The weeks and months that followed were long and arduous. Between my practice, the operating room, and my laboratory at the university, I rarely got home in time to see Linda and the kids before dinner and the kids' 10:00 p.m. bedtime. Justin was only eleven but very much like a teenager. He could always be found either on the phone or sleeping. Fortunately, he was an excellent student and had a heart of gold. Diana was my princess. At eight, she already had me wrapped around her finger. She had a way of making me melt just by putting her arm around me while I was sitting down or asking, "Daddy, could you help me with my homework?" I knew full well I could never really help her with anything. She was a whip; she knew all the answers. It was just her way of making sure I would spend some special time with her. What a young lady. She sure made me feel guilty at times.

Linda was at her breaking point. Having worked many years developing her own consulting business, she was just beginning to savor the fruits of her labors. However, life isn't always fair. Her mom was now in the end stage of Alzheimer's disease, her dad was suffering from disabling back problems, and of course the kids were as demanding as ever. She somehow seemed to handle it all—until recently. I had also noticed a change of late in Linda. She was always very tired and occasionally impatient with the children. This was quite unusual for her. At first, I thought it was the sheer magnitude of her responsibilities: taking care of her parents while attending to the children as well as her business. However, I had noted that she appeared pale and nauseous, particularly in the morning. If she hadn't had her tubes tied after the birth of our daughter, I would have thought she was pregnant. I hadn't mentioned my concern to Linda, but I was worried something was wrong. I had planned to have her evaluated but kept putting it off, hoping her symptoms would end on their own.

That was always the way doctors had been—and will probably always be: less concerned about themselves and more concerned about the health of their families and patients. I didn't think it was entirely altruistic. Rather, it was a function of knowing too much, confronting their own mortality, and not wanting any bad things to happen to the ones they loved and needed so much. I also felt that part of their concern stemmed from not wanting to do anything that would harm their family. Therefore, their judgment was always clouded when dealing with the health problems of family. But this had been going on too long with Linda: four weeks now, and it was getting worse. A sure sign of a real problem was that it was not getting better. I would make sure she made an appointment with her gynecologist, the only doctor she had. In fact, I would call him myself and make sure that he would see her soon.

Linda's gynecologist, Dr. Dan Cleary, was on vacation, so she had made an appointment with his partner, Dr. Harvey Princeton. She would have waited for Dan to return, but I knew she just wasn't feeling right and wanted to be seen sooner rather than later. Harvey was a great guy. He brought both our children into this world and always had a smile on his face. However, he had very set priorities: family and self. He was a devoted father and husband, and although he always wanted (and had) the finer things in life, he would forsake it all for a day on the golf course. He negotiated into his contract to have one day a week off for personal issues, even though I'm sure it cost him tens of thousands of dollars a year in compensation.

Linda was very nervous about her doctor's appointment, more so than she had been in many years. She had a great sense about her body, and that made me also concerned. Shortly after we were married—I believe she was twenty-five at the time—she felt she was gaining weight and noted bloating in her abdomen. Most women would probably relate this to their menstrual cycle, but Linda knew this wasn't so. She had gone immediately to her gynecologist and was operated on three days later for what turned out to be a football-size ovarian cyst. Fortunately, it was benign, but I was never more scared. The realization that I could never really protect her, or anyone I loved, hit home, really hard. It certainly gave me a different outlook on life and our human frailty. I was also quite concerned about what was going on.

I received a call from Harvey at 2:20 p.m.

"Barry?"

"Hi, Harvey. How's Linda?"

"You won't believe it! She has an ectopic pregnancy."

"What? She had a tubal ligation."

"She has a gestational sac in her pelvis just outside her remaining ovary and an hCG of two thousand."

"How do you think it occurred?"

"Probably a low-grade infection at the site of the suture resulted in a small opening of the tube allowing sperm to exit and fertilize the egg in her pelvis."

It sounded plausible, but I wondered why she hadn't had other symptoms, like a fever or pain, before this time. "How are you going to treat it?"

"Given the blood level of hCG, I thought we would give methotrexate. If the value doesn't decrease in a couple days, we can surgically remove it. There's also a collection of fluid around the ectopic. I'm not quite sure what it is, but I'll keep watching it."

"How's Linda taking the news?"

"I think she's relieved. She was expecting the worst."

"Me too. Is she there? Can I speak with her?"

"She just left. She had to pick up Diana from school and said she would see you at home."

"Thanks so much, Harvey. I suppose you'll want to see her back tomorrow?"

"You bet. Every day for the next week. And by the way, Barry..."

"Yeah, Harvey?"

"You might think about a vasectomy!"

"Great. That's just what I wanted to hear." I was so happy to hear it was just an ectopic pregnancy and not something more dreadful that my manly fear of being cut "down there" didn't sink in. I must have performed hundreds of vasectomies myself. The patients routinely did well and were all so much braver than I was. I was given encouragement—and many off-color comments about my resistance—by my buddy Larry Weiss at the racquetball club during our weekly Wednesday evening games. Larry had had a vasectomy after his third child. Linda and I had decided that two children were just perfect for us and that either I would have a vasectomy, or she would have a tubal ligation after the pregnancy with Diana. As it turned out, Linda needed a C-section and had her fallopian tubes ligated. I felt that my resistance to having a vasectomy in some way contributed to her having to undergo the C-section. However, with this failure, we needed to again consider a means of contraception. I guess some higher authority decided it was time I live up to my husbandly responsibility.

It was February 1993 when we received the gene sequencer at the lab. A Silicon Valley firm had designed this desktop model for the pharmaceutical industry that only big pharma could afford. We were the first university lab to receive one. We were stunned when we received an e-mail and delivery date for ours, donated by an anonymous benefactor. I suspected Bob was the generous benefactor.

The SE40 sequencer was the latest in the series of sequencers designed to automate the identification of nucleotides. We needed to find a single nucleotide change in a gene controlling sperm production. Nucleotides are the building blocks of DNA. This is important since the genetic information of a cell is stored in the form of DNA. A change in the character of even a single nucleotide can result in a genetic mutation with life-changing effects. However, there are over three billion nucleotides in the twenty-three paired chromosomes of the human genome. To find a single nucleotide mutation would have been an impossible undertaking without the SE40.

When we received the SE40, the bill of lading indicated the purchaser as ReproMed. I then recalled that ReproMed was the ID on the prior phone call from Bob. I needed to speak with Bob about this and thank him.

I tried searching for information on ReproMed. Unfortunately, it was a private company with little public information. Only the address and year of incorporation.

We put the sequencer to work immediately on sequencing DNA we isolated from Bob. With this sequencer, we could determine the structure that coded for a unique protein produced in Bob's cells that had a similar chemical structure to testosterone; however, it appeared to block the effect that testosterone normally had on cells in the testes.

Bob stopped by to see how the work was proceeding. I was always amazed by his core knowledge and his thirst for learning all he could. I needed to thank him first for arranging for the sequencer.

"Bob," I said, "the bill of lading for the sequencer listed ReproMed as the purchaser. I also remembered you had called me from that number. Did you buy the machine for us?" I asked.

"Dr. Gifford, you are quite a detective," he said, trying to hold back a smile. "I was asked to be an investor in ReproMed, and I might have convinced some of the principals to support your research a bit. I convinced them that it would ultimately benefit their bottom line to make this philanthropic donation to the university's research. We specified in our gift to the university that it would be used for this specific purpose. I hope you don't mind."

"Not at all," I quickly responded. "The more help we have the better." He obviously did not want to discuss this topic further and quickly changed the subject.

"Dr. Gifford, I hope you don't mind me coming over to learn a little more about all this."

"Are you kidding? It's great to have you here. We're trying to isolate the hormone we believe is present in the tissue we took from you during surgery." I could see by the furrow in Bob's brow and dazed look in his eyes that he was deep in thought. "Do you know much about hormones?"

"Only that there are many types, each having a unique job."

"Exactly right!" I said. "Hormones work by activating synthesis of specific proteins inside the cell. The proteins that are produced can then do their job, whether it is building muscle mass or stimulating sperm production. To do this, the hormone must first be transported into the cell and then bind to specific sites. It does this by binding to a special protein molecule called a receptor. There is a receptor for every hormone in the body. However, only the target cells—those cells that the hormone works on—have receptors specific for a given hormone."

"But how does this relate to sperm production?" Bob responded with renewed interest.

"Sperm production in the testes is very much like a production line for car assembly. An immature sperm enters the line as a round blob of nutritional and genetic material, and other cells lining the tubules in the testes reshape it into a tadpole-like form. These supporting cells are known as sertoli cells and are just like the computer-controlled robotics along an assembly line that builds a car. Testosterone turns on the robots that produce sperm and allows the sperm to mature.

"We suspect that the substance we hope to isolate is like testosterone in that it binds to the receptor on the sertoli cells, effectively blocking testosterone from binding. However, unlike testosterone, our substance is unable to turn on the robots and therefore actually prevents maturation of sperm. What is even more exciting is that this substance is specific only for the receptors on the sertoli cells where sperm mature. It doesn't seem to have the ability to block testosterone's binding to any other receptors. The importance of this is a pharmacologist's dream. A receptor blocker with such specificity would make side effects very unlikely."

"Unbelievable," Bob exclaimed, hardly containing his excitement. "I can see how that could be a commercially valuable."

"It really is. We also needed a name for this substance. We thought Tesbloc would be perfect for a drug that could block testosterone. What do you think?" I asked, knowing his keen sense of marketing.

"Sounds good to me," he stated hesitantly. "Give me some time to think about it."

As I was telling this story to Bob, I felt something wasn't right. I couldn't put my finger on it, but as I was relating the findings to Bob, something was missing. I'm sure it would come to me. I just needed a little time. We still had a lot of work ahead: characterization of the substance, testing in the lab, and animal studies. All this had to be done prior to human trials. This would take years. Plenty of time to find out what might be missing.

20

EUREKA

Bob's semen analysis demonstrated a single moving sperm at sixteen weeks after surgery. Unbelievable! Even though only one motile sperm was found, this was a finding of colossal proportions. We had a substance that reversibly stopped sperm production—a reversible male contraceptive! We just needed to isolate and identify it.

This hormone was capable of completely and reversibly suppressing sperm production. If I could prove that use of this isolate also inhibited spermatogenesis in normal men, I would have developed a reversible male contraceptive—a development of major importance and unknown fortunes. Not that I would see any money from this since it was developed in the university lab, and they would own any patent. At least that was what Charles had told me. However, on the bright side, subsequent funding for my research would be much easier to obtain.

We still needed to start Bob on his injectable medications. I called him to give him the news. He answered on the first ring. He likely anticipated my phone call.

"Bob, great news! We have a sperm in your specimen," I said with elation.

"Wow! That is fantastic! Do you still want me to start the medications?" Bob inquired.

"It really is. A proof of our theory. Yes, you should start the HCG and return in four weeks for blood tests as we discussed. Your blood tests showed a low production of LH by your pituitary. It can use the boost," I said.

"Will do, Doc!" Bob replied.

I thought back to the first time I met Bob prior to seeing him as a patient. It was at a hospital cocktail hour at the Gottersman Research Pavilion opening ceremony. I was asked, along with two of my colleagues, to give a short talk on my research on genetic variations in reproductive medicine. The goal was to attract donations from wealthy benefactors. Bob appeared to be quite interested in my talk and approached me afterward to ask several insightful questions. I thought for sure he was a scientist. We spent much of the evening discussing my research. We struck up a friendship and met up again several times for coffee over the next few months. The discussions would move from science to sports to politics to family and back to science. Always back to science.

I found out during our talks that Bob Ludlow was a very wealthy man with a high-profile job. Bob's given name was Robert S. Ludlow Jr. His family and friends referred to him as Bob and his late dad as the governor. His dad was the founder of Ludlow Enterprises Inc., a manufacturer of sophisticated electronic circuitry. Following his dad's death, Bob became the patriarch of his family, always caring for his siblings. His mother had died giving birth to him, and his father remarried. His younger half sister, Lynn, was married to a physician, Mark Niebling, a kind and giving man twenty years her senior. However, he did not have a mind for financial matters. His half brother, Jack, was the black sheep of the family. He was brilliant, for sure, but without direction. Jack had completed his undergraduate training and a law degree at Harvard. Afterward, he spent two years traveling through Europe, finding his calling, as he would always point out.

Jack had been a bachelor of the nineties, jumping into bed with any woman he met without any thought of consequences.

Bob was the antithesis of his brother, Jack. He was a devoted husband with an uncanny ability to make complex business transactions. He was also plagued by a medical issue that he hesitated to discuss with me. However, over the several months of our meetings, he started to feel more comfortable opening up. He stated he had been feeling depressed lately, which had affected his performance at work and strained his relationship with his wife. He had also been drinking much more.

He said that that the major focus of his depression was a fertility issue being treated by Dr. Dexter Brunswick. He admitted that his brother-in-law had asked him to get a second opinion and that he had recommended me. He had not mentioned at the time that he was also given my name by Brunswick himself. There was something more there, though. I detected that Bob had strong emotions for this man. I was not sure whether it was hatred or fear. I didn't know what Dr. Brunswick had done, but I planned to find out.

Bob had asked me if I could review Dr. Brunswick's records and see if I could help. Bob was unaware of the adverse actions that I have heard involving Brunswick. I had just been contacted by a malpractice attorney to review a case involving Dr. Brunswick. The attorney had told me on the phone that he had done inappropriate surgery on his client. I refused to be involved, simply stating that I felt it would be a conflict of interest for me since I was his local competition. I also heard through a well-connected colleague of mine that the county peer-review committee and the state office of professional medical conduct had both brought charges against Dr. Brunswick. In addition, a recent newspaper article stated that the tax department was investigating him for a company that he was involved in. However, he was quite adept at manipulating the system. I had little confidence that these investigations would result in significant sanctions.

I first met Dr. Brunswick when doing my male infertility fellowship at Metropolitan University Hospital. He was a tall, lanky man with a well-groomed mustache, and the thick brown plastic of his horn-rimmed glasses highlighted his beady blue eyes. He consistently wore dark suits, white shirts, and bow ties. He had completed his male fertility fellowship at the prestigious Boston City Hospital the year prior before joining the staff at MUH as a private practice attending. He returned to Boston several times during the year to oversee papers that he had medical students and residents work on for him. He was a master of getting others to do work assigned to him. The gossip from Boston was that the female office staff would avoid being alone with him. It was not that his words or actions were inappropriate. It was just an uncomfortable feeling they had when he was nearby.

I could not understand why Brunswick's practice had grown over the past few years. No doubt he was talented, but he was a vile man with an arrogant personality and questionable ethics. Residents hated to be on call when one of his patients was sent for admission. I remember when I was in my first year of fellowship, and Dr. Brunswick was a first-year attending, he would call me prior to his patient arriving at the hospital to make sure that I knew exactly what he wanted done on his patient. At first I thought this was completely appropriate—what with him being senior to me—but I was not savvy in the ways of the "private slick," as the other residents used to refer to him. What I found out was that this was his way of justifying a surgical procedure. He would admit the patient with minimal symptoms and order a battery of tests. If the tests confirmed his clinical impression, he then had justification to operate. And if they didn't, no matter; a surgical exploration was then needed for diagnosis. He couldn't lose!

21

MORNING

Friday, August 4, 1995

A big, burly sanitation worker awakened me. "Hey, buddy...You all right?"

Sure I was. I was lying in a pool of blood, and I felt as if my head had been placed in a vise. My wrist and lower back were hurting, but otherwise I was fine. I could see blood oozing through my shirt. "Yeah, I'm fine," I echoed with a raspy voice. I could feel my throat encased in dried blood. "Do you see my car keys?"

"Don't think you should be driving right now, buddy."

He was right. I had this loud ringing in my ears...and that headache. "You know where I can get a cab?" That was the last thing I remembered until I awoke in the ambulance.

The office parking lot was only a few blocks away from the MUH emergency room. The ambulance ride to the hospital was only a few minutes, but it seemed like hours. I knew I should be examined, but like most physicians, I felt I could take care of anything that could happen to me. My friend Dr. Martin Kennedy greeted me at the emergency department.

"Hey, Barry, what the hell happened?"

I heard Marty's voice but still couldn't focus on what he was asking. Marty was a great friend—always there when I needed him. I found myself drifting in and out of consciousness.

Marty's wife, Clara, was a nurse—a beautiful Southern belle. They met while he was an intern at MUH. It was love at first sight. However, they'd been trying to conceive now for three years. Clara had been through the gauntlet of fertility testing: examinations, blood testing, biopsies of her uterine lining, X-ray studies of her fallopian tubes, and injections in almost every part of her body to produce more eggs. Still no success. Only then did someone ask if her husband had ever been tested. And wouldn't you know—a single semen analysis on her husband highlighted the problem. He had too few sperm in his specimen, and those that were there weren't moving very well.

It had always disturbed me how doctors—and good doctors, at that—had such monocular vision. They were so involved with their own specialties that they often failed to see the larger picture. Oncologists felt that toxic drugs were the way to treat a cancer patient, while radiologists felt that radiation was the best way to go. It all depended on whom the patient saw first. In the fertility field, things were no different. Experts in female fertility, known as reproductive endocrinologists, felt that you started with the woman, and all you needed from the man was a sperm. The male fertility expert, usually a urologist who had subspecialized in male fertility, felt that treating the male was the best way to proceed. If only doctors could work together more often. In this instance, Clara would have been spared the discomfort and the cost of testing if a simple sperm test had been done early on in her evaluation.

Clara had finally gotten Marty to come in to see me. In fact, he was supposed to come to my office for an appointment today.

I was beginning to focus again.

"Hey, Barry, did you hear me? I asked what happened," Marty repeated much louder with also a bit more concern in his voice. I was now beginning to focus.

"I heard you. You don't have to shout. I guess we'll have to reschedule your appointment," I replied as my head pounded.

"No shit, man. From what I heard, you're lucky you're not dead." Marty always knew just what to say. "I gotta get you an MRI and see if there's anything left in that ugly-looking head of yours. Barry, does Linda know you're here?"

Linda! She probably had the entire county police force out looking for me. I needed to get to a phone.

"Marty...please get to a phone...need to let Linda know I'm alive."

Marty dragged over the handset from the wall phone and dialed my house.

"Hello, Linda? It's me. I'm fine." All I heard was sobbing on the other end. "Honey, I'm really OK."

"Barry," Linda said, her voice cracking. "I was so scared. What happened? Where are you?"

"Honey, I'm at the University Hospital emergency department. Marty's taking care of me. After you get the kids off to school—" There was a dial tone. I knew Linda was on her way. My head hurt so much I couldn't concentrate. Also, my left wrist ached. I felt like I had been dragged by the wrist.

"Marty, do you know where my briefcase and files are?"

"Your briefcase? With all that's happened to you, you can only think of your briefcase? I put it in your locker."

"Marty, what about the files I was carrying?" I wasn't feeling well. Just talking made my head spin and pound.

"I didn't see any files. What's the difference, anyway? You're alive, aren't you?" Marty was a real friend. He knew by the urgency in my voice that I was troubled. "Don't be so concerned, Barry. Files can be replaced."

"Damn it," I said, as they began taking me off for my MRI.

"Damn what?" Marty repeated.

"I don't understand. They took it!"

"Took what?" Marty asked.

I didn't even answer him. Instead, I pleaded with Marty to bring my briefcase to me.

22

RECOVERY

Saturday, August 5, 1995

It was Saturday morning when I was discharged. I was given an appointment for a Monday morning follow-up with a neurologist who examined me while I was hospitalized. They had kept me two nights in the hospital for observation.

The darkly stained oak door of my Victorian-style house felt exceedingly heavy as I opened it.

"Daddy!" Diana exclaimed as she ran to embrace me with tears rolling down her rosy cheeks. Diana was a petite eight-year-old. But so adorable with her long blond hair and hazel eyes.

"Why the tears, my princess?" I asked.

"Mommy said that you were hurt," she responded. So sweet, so sensitive. Just like Linda.

"I feel fine. I just need to rest for a day or so," I said.

"A day or so!" Linda retorted as she entered closely behind me, trying to support me.

"Marty said three days and bed rest today. I am going to make sure of it."

"But, Linda," I responded, "the MRI was normal."

"If you heard what Marty said, the MRI is not able to diagnose a concussion. Which is what he suspects you had," Linda continued.

"He wants you to stay lying down for twenty-four hours and wants me to check on you every hour to make sure you are alert."

"Well, I guess I will finally get some time to spend with the kids," I said as I smiled.

As if on cue, my eleven-year-old son, Justin, pounded down the stairs. "Hey, Dad, you OK?"

"Just fine. Gotta rest a bit, and I'll be back to normal. How's school today?" I asked.

"Not bad—just have some math homework," he responded.

"Need any help?" I asked.

"Just finishing it now. Maybe you can check it over?" he asked.

"Sure, bring it down," I responded.

Justin was a great student. We never had to remind him to do his homework. Unlike most boys in his sixth-grade class. If there was one bright light in this terrible ordeal, it was being able to spend time with Linda and my kids. I was proud of the practice I had been building but had been so consumed by work that I didn't get time to spend with my family. I'd wanted to change that for some time now. The parking lot assault was a life-changing event for me. I vowed I would start changing my priorities before it was too late, and the kids were grown.

I recalled my childhood as very different. I could remember that my parents always made time to be with me. Maybe a little too much. Ah, the plight of being an only child. Dad worked as a financial consultant. He was up early but always made it home to cook dinner. And Mom didn't mind. Mom worked from home as a speech pathologist. We lived less than a mile from the public school. Just short of the distance required to take the bus but a bit too long to walk, at least when I was in elementary school. She would arrange the parents' carpool. As it turned out, she was usually the one driving; most of the other parents lacked her sense of responsibility.

My adolescence was the time when I got to know my dad. He wanted to spend as much time with me as he could. He introduced me to all types of sporting activities and encouraged me to join school sports teams. And he was there at every game to support me. He was always available for a pickup basketball game or to drive my friends and me to play baseball at the school field on the weekends. Unfortunately, he passed away in his fifties from a stroke. Mom understandably took his death very hard. But somehow, she was able to pull herself back together and expand her career.

As it turned out, Dad had a rare genetic mutation that no one had picked up. They called it an inborn error. A defect in a gene that caused that gene to make a different protein with oftentimes deadly effects. In my dad's case, it caused a clogging of blood vessels in his brain, which was followed by a seizure and then death within minutes. Little was known about it at the time, but it was probably also related to the problems they had having me.

I was in college at the time of his death. This event was probably what made me go into medicine. I was planning on going into finance to follow in Dad's footsteps. But his sudden and unexpected death caused an abrupt change in my career and launched me into the study of genetics and male fertility. I wanted to make a difference.

I looked over Justin's homework. He didn't need my help. Linda was checking on me every hour as she said she would.

"Linda, I am going to take a nap. I feel exhausted."

"And I will keep checking on you each hour!" she echoed.

"Would not think otherwise. Sorry I gave you such a scare," I responded.

"I am more concerned about why they attacked you. The police started questioning me at the hospital, but I knew nothing. They wanted to spend more time speaking with you. However, you were still recovering, and the doctors thought it best to wait a little. They said they would look at the area around where you were found and return to talk to you, possibly today or over the next few days," she said. "I will wake you when they arrive."

I couldn't stop thinking about why Bob's chart was taken and why I wasn't killed. My immediate thought was that Brunswick was somehow involved. But why? These were only copies of the records that Bob had. It just didn't make sense why anyone would risk so much to take so little. Then I remembered the woman's voice saying, "The chart, not the briefcase." Maybe taking the chart was just a ruse to divert attention from their real purpose, but what was the real purpose? Possibly they were after my research notebook that was in my briefcase? But how could they know about that? My wrist was still hurting.

I kept my appointment with the neurologist on Monday morning. I had no choice. Medical staff regulations did not allow me to work until cleared by the neurologist. He said I was doing great. Just would not clear me for work. He would reevaluate me at the end of the week. At least I was encouraged by his saying "…and possibly clear you to return to your research responsibilities and seeing patients."

"And surgery?" I asked.

"Dr. Gifford, you sustained a pretty significant concussion. You were unconscious for at least six hours," he stated. "You are lucky you didn't die or sustain permanent brain injury." I don't think he could have been more melodramatic.

I considered this overkill. I was feeling well. My headache was much better and controlled by medications, even though I found myself sleeping a good bit of the time. My thoughts continued to be consumed by the attack. I tried to recall events leading up to it that might be related. Linda's concern about why they attacked me was disturbing. I kept returning to Bob and his encounter with Dexter Brunswick. My most vivid memories were during my short naps during the day.

I arrived home before noon. I was tired and went to the couch on the main floor to lie down. It was 3:00 p.m. when Justin answered the door.

"Hey, Dad, there is a real detective here to see you!" he exclaimed as he excitedly ran to me. I was on the couch in the living room, not far from the front door.

"Please show him in," I requested. "Head is still hurting a bit. Think I'll just lie here," I responded.

Detective O'Brien entered. He was probably six feet tall but seemed a lot taller from my vantage point. He had dark hair combed back from the front. With his large neck and broad shoulders, his physique was more that of an athlete than a detective. "How are you feeling, Doc?" he inquired.

"Getting better, thanks. Still have a pounding headache, though," I responded, thinking he didn't sound Irish.

"You look a lot better now than you did in the hospital," he said.

"Sorry, don't remember much from the hospital," I responded. "Did I speak with you there? I was really out of it."

"If you don't mind, I would like to review the event with you. Think you feel well enough to talk?" he asked.

"Sure. Have you found out anything?" I asked.

"The cameras in the parking lot showed a panel truck and the two individuals near you, which matches with your statement in the hospital. But the ambient light was too little to make out the color of the truck or identify the two people. It also seemed like they knew where the cameras were since we could only make out the back of their heads. We also saw a third person who stayed near the truck. Not sure whether male or female. Any idea who that could be?" Detective O'Brien asked.

I suspected from Detective O'Brien's inflection in his voice that he knew something he was not saying.

"No idea," I stated. "Only two voices that I could make out before I lost consciousness. Wow! A third person was there, just watching. Does that mean anything?"

"Probably less likely that it was a random act," he replied.

"I'll keep you updated with anything I find out," he said. "Please let me know if you remember anything else."

Detective O'Brien had stayed for about an hour. He covered every moment of that day. His voice was always calm and professional. He was also very considerate in asking me if I needed a break or if he should come back another time to continue the discussion. He appeared truly concerned with trying to get to the bottom of this and find those responsible. I also felt that he wanted to protect me and my family. However, from what or from whom he did not say.

There was something very familiar about the detective. I could not put my finger on it. I had a good feeling about him though.

23

THE SETUP

Wednesday, September 6, 1995

A loud knock on the door awakened me. I glanced at the clock. It was almost 2:30 a.m. I knew this couldn't be good news. I had to walk down a long hallway on the way to the staircase that spiraled to the main floor. The front door, which had a window that overlooked the front porch, was right underneath me in the hallway. I could see a police car in front with flashing lights. My heart started pounding. *What was this all about?* I wondered.

It was unusually cold this late summer night. A hail storm was forecast. The heat was on in the house. I could hear the valves on the boiler hissing as the steam percolated up from the basement. The main floor was always a bit warmer than the upstairs. I suppose it was the nature of steam heat. However, as I approached the front door, I felt a chill go right through me.

I reached the door and began to open it, not realizing that what I was about to encounter would change my life forever.

"Are you Dr. Barry Gifford?" asked an unshaven man with piercing brown eyes.

"Yes, I am," I replied with obvious concern.

"I'm Detective Tollins, and this is my partner, Detective O'Brien, of the One Hundred Sixth Precinct, homicide division." Two uniformed cops accompanied him. "We would like to ask you some questions."

I was somewhat relived to see Detective O'Brien, although this was short-lived. "Sure," I said, thinking this wouldn't be a bad thing to do.

"Is this your watch?" Detective Tollins asked. He seemed to know the answer as he showed me an exact duplicate of the Seiko watch Linda had given me for my thirtieth birthday. However, the watch they showed me was in a plastic bag and appeared bloodstained. *Why were they showing me this?* I thought.

"No, but it looks exactly like the one I have upstairs on my dresser," I replied. "What is this all about?" A part of me didn't really want to know the answer.

"How can you be sure this isn't yours?" Detective O'Brien asked sincerely.

"Well," I started to explain while holding the bag closer to examine the watch. As I turned it over, my knees weakened, my face flushed, and I felt like I couldn't breathe. The inscription read, "All my love, all my life, Linda." Could it really be mine? "This could be mine," I told the detective. "Let me get the watch I have upstairs to compare." I handed the watch back to the detective. I glanced at Detective O'Brien as I turned to proceed upstairs. He noted my distress.

"Just one moment," Detective Tollins said. "I have a warrant to search these premises." He handed me papers. "I'll accompany you to your room." He gave the other uniformed officers directions to search the rest of the house.

The walk upstairs seemed interminable. The noise had awakened Linda, and she was starting to descend the stairs as I was going back to our room.

"What's going on, Barry?" she asked with an obvious tremor in her voice.

"Don't quite know yet, honey. They showed me a watch that looks identical to the one you gave me." Linda always knew when I was really concerned about something. She approached me and tightly grabbed my left arm. It's funny—everything felt much better then.

As I entered the room, I saw my watch sitting on the dresser as I had left it. I was starting to feel my heart slow. However, as I reached for it, I felt a queasiness that began in the pit of my stomach and traveled down deep into my soul. The watch felt very heavy in my hands. I was concerned about what I would find when I looked at the back. My palms were sweating as I turned the watch over. No inscription. I froze in place. I felt as if I were disassociated from my body.

Detective Tollins asked, "Where were you between eight p.m. and ten p.m. last evening?"

"Wednesday evening, I usually have my weekly racquetball game," I replied.

"Is there someone who can corroborate your presence?" Tollins inquired.

"Not really. I have not been playing with my buddy since my head injury. I just practice by myself," I answered.

"Why? What happened?" I asked.

"Dr. Gifford," Detective Tollins stated with an arrogant demeanor. "You are under arrest for the murder of Bob Ludlow. You have the right—"

"What?" I shouted. "No…it can't be. Bob can't be dead."

24

PROLOGUE TO THE TRIAL

Wednesday, September 6, 1995

The cold rain pelted the windows of my cell. It was small, about eight feet by ten feet, but it could have been even smaller. I had not moved since I was taken there in the early morning. I was frozen in disbelief. Torn from my family for a crime I didn't commit. And Linda. I didn't get the chance to see her, to let her know it wasn't me. Why was all this happening? Maybe it was just a dream. I'll wake up and be back in my bed.

"Hey, Doc. Someone here to see you."

I was shocked back into reality. "Hi, Larry," I said sheepishly. "Guess this isn't a bad dream."

I was glad to see Larry Weiss. He was a good friend, my college roommate, and my racquetball partner. Besides graduating law school summa cum laude and being a partner at the best legal defense firm in town, he could be trusted to get to the bottom of this.

"Barry, Linda called me as they left your house," Larry stated. "Did you give a statement to the police?"

"Just in response to my whereabouts on the night I was mugged."

"What did you say?"

"Just that I left my home at seven o'clock after the kids were asleep and went to practice by myself at the racquetball club. I just said my racquetball partner couldn't make it. Did not say it was you I usually play with."

"Was that all you said?"

"I don't recall anything else."

"Good, just don't say any more unless I'm present."

"Larry, what the hell is going on? I didn't murder Bob. We were friends. Someone must have taken my watch and exchanged it for a duplicate."

"Barry, they're saying you noticed it was missing after you killed Bob Ludlow and bought a new one to replace it."

"How could they know about my watch and what was engraved on the back?" I mused. "I think I know how they did it. These must be the same people that mugged me in the parking. Got a look at my watch at that time. They then knew about my scheduled racquetball games on Wednesdays and followed me. They waited for a day when I was alone, which as you know occurs at least once a month with your schedule, and switched the watch, which I kept in my locker when I was playing," I explained.

"Sounds convoluted and difficult to prove," Larry responded.

"How was he murdered?" I asked, not really wanting to hear the answer.

"Bludgeoned in the head with a heavy object. Seems he knew his attacker," Larry added.

"Why do you say that?" Bob asked.

"No sign of a struggle. The strange part is that it occurred two blocks from your office late in the evening," Larry said.

What was Bob doing near his office at that time? What could have lured him there, and how did he come to have my watch? I was full of questions but had very few answers. "What happens now?" I asked.

"We see the judge. I hope he'll set bail, and we can get you home. I gotta say, the evidence presented in the police report is pretty substantial."

"Larry, you do believe that I didn't kill Bob? Don't you?"

"Of course, Barry. I just meant that we have a lot of work to do before trial."

"Trial? I just want to go home. Can I get out of here tonight?"

"It looks like you'll be arraigned in the morning."

"What do I do about my surgery cases?"

"Surgery cases! Barry, I know you care about your patients, but this is one time you must take care of yourself first."

I knew Larry was right but couldn't help thinking.

"Also, I don't quite know how to put this, but with being arrested for murder, your privileges at the hospital will most likely be immediately suspended."

"Can they do that?"

"Well, the bylaws of the medical staff refer to moral character and allude to the process of termination of medical staff privileges. However, whether they can or they can't, they will do it. Not much we can do about it right now. We have bigger problems to deal with."

My stomach was in knots. I couldn't concentrate. I kept thinking about Bob and who had murdered him. Linda was holding it together. But just barely. I had been released on bond upon giving up title to my house to secure my appearance in court the day after next. My house, my life, it was unbelievable. Accused of murdering a man I respected and considered to be a friend? How could this be happening? Who was behind this conspiracy? The clock was ticking, and my whole life seemed to stop.

Larry was right; the hospital had suspended my privileges upon hearing of my arrest. It might not have been allowed without due process, but try and fight them. I was wondering if I would still have a practice left when my patients heard of my arrest. And Linda. How were she and the kids going to handle the house and their lives if I wasn't around? No, I shouldn't be thinking that way. I'm not guilty.

I didn't murder him. Funny, I sounded like a B movie where the accused says, "I didn't do it," and the other inmates say, "Yeah, we're all innocent too." But I really was! Damn it. If I could only get my hands on—

My thoughts kept returning to Dr. Brunswick. There were too many questions and few answers. Could he be responsible for Bob's murder? What could be his motive? Why would he kill his patient?

Larry and I were scheduled to meet, prior to my arrest, to discuss commercialization based on the discovery of Tesbloc—the substance I had isolated and sequenced from Bob's accessory ovaries appeared to suppress sperm production. The hospital attorneys were working on the patent. Larry had worked with them on past patents, and they asked for his help on the commercialization piece. I kept thinking that my evaluation of Bob, together with the surgical and laboratory findings, could prove very incriminating for Dr. Brunswick. Could this be his motive?

However, if clinical studies confirmed our initial findings, Tesbloc might be the first oral male contraceptive—a multibillion-dollar market! We needed to protect our interests in this.

I guess I hadn't really understood the significance of my work until I opened the paper the next morning. There on the front page for all the world to see was the headline, "Medical Breakthrough: Dr. Dexter Brunswick Develops First Effective Male Contraceptive." I read on: "Dr. Dexter Brunswick, a noted expert in male reproductive disorders, reports on the identification of a naturally released substance from glands in men born with abnormalities of their reproductive system that reversibly prevents sperm production."

I couldn't believe my eyes! My work, my data now on the front page of the *Times*. How could he even consider reporting this? How could he hope to present my data as his own? He probably thought that people would perceive publication of this story in the lay press as indisputable proof of his claim of originality.

But how did he even know of my work and get my data? Was there was someone on my team working for Dr. Brunswick or at least willing to sell information. But who? I couldn't get the thought out of my mind. Someone I knew and trusted could be conspiring with Brunswick. I guess I've always been naive.

If Dr. Brunswick was corrupt enough to steal my data, he was also smart enough to know that he couldn't carry on this charade for long. The surgery, the research, and the manuscripts were all evidence of prior art, all separately documented and all with independent witnesses to this work. What did he hope to gain? More importantly, how does one deal with a man with such a lack of ethics? Answers to these questions were not long in coming.

25

THE LETTER

The rain had finally ended. It had been raining off and on for the better part of two weeks. The sky remained gray, however. I had two hours before Larry was to pick me up for the deposition. I had only been to one of them in my professional life. I remembered it as being intimidating. For the lawyers, it was just another day at the office. To me, it was an unwelcome experience that I met with apprehension and a twinge of fear. Being calm in surgery was the antithesis of my composure when the individuals interrogating me were convinced I was guilty of a crime I didn't commit. I was not looking forward to the awkward feeling of not being in control.

I was still in my boxers and undershirt. Linda had not left my side since we returned home. I couldn't sleep, and she slept with one eye open. She really didn't want to leave me alone, but I knew she had promised to take her friend Ellen to the station while Ellen's car was in for repair. Linda always kept her promises.

"Honey, I'll be back in just a few minutes. Are you sure you'll be all right?" She gave me a kiss and a hug. I didn't want her to let go.

"I'll be fine." I felt very vulnerable. I hoped I was right. Linda left through the garage door. I felt cold and alone.

It was so hard to get myself going. My legs felt heavy. My stomach was in a knot. I just wanted to crawl under the covers and sleep for a long, long time. I was hoping against hope that I would wake up and this bad dream would be gone.

The newspaper should be here by now, I thought. I should find out what the press was saying about me. I probably shouldn't care, but I couldn't help it. I walked through the kitchen to retrieve it. As I approached the front door, I noticed a letter pushed underneath it. It had no stamp or return address. I grabbed my raincoat from the closet next to the front door and stepped into my loafers. I exited to pick up the paper that had been thrown into the bushes, as usual. It always made me laugh how inaccurate the paper deliverer was. It almost never ended up near the front door.

It felt weird to be home on a Tuesday at eight in the morning. Usually I'd have finished rounds and been starting my first case in the operating room. As obsessive as I was, I kept checking on my patients by calling a colleague who was covering my patients while I was on a forced leave from my practice. I felt my emotional state changed as if a switch was flipped. Just thinking about this injustice made me mad. No one had the right to take away my life like this. Something I'd worked so hard to achieve. I was also feeling sorry for myself. I sat at the kitchen table and looked at the letter. Large block letters were typed on the back: "Dr. Barry Gifford. Confidential."

I slit the letter open with the bread knife from the table.

> *Dr. Gifford,*
>
> *I am risking it all to write this. They're watching both of us. I was there when it happened. It didn't need to be this way, but he wanted it all. I was powerless to stop him. You must believe me.*
>
> *I could not live with myself knowing the crime that has occurred and knowing that I was involved. You know the enemy of whom I speak. He is an evil and vile man. I warn you: do not underestimate his reach. He has mercenaries ready to act—and act they will—against you and your family and all*

others who come between him and his goals. He is untouchable. Do not trust the friendly stranger. I have said enough. My life will not be long.

May you be steadfast in your position. I only ask for your forgiveness.

Your ally

I sat motionless. I felt a bit queasy as my pounding heart quickened.

26

THE PRELIMINARY HEARING

Tuesday, September 12, 1995

The conference room had twelve Chesterfield leather chairs surrounding a large oval cherry-mahogany table. Fine art adorned a small area of the far wall nestled between burled mahogany bookshelves overfilled with legal fare. It was made to impress and unnerve. Three attorneys were seated opposite me with a court reporter to my left. Larry was sitting immediately to my right. Judge Harvey entered from his chambers. He was not at all what I expected. He was a well-groomed man in his forties with a short, cropped mustache and no jacket. His shirtsleeves were rolled up to his elbows, and he wore wide, bold paisley suspenders. The purpose of this preliminary hearing was simple: my attorney would register a plea of not guilty on my behalf and see if all parties were ready to go to trial. If so, a trial date would be set.

"Dr. Gifford," Judge Harvey bellowed with a deep voice much more senior than his apparent age. "Have you been apprised of the charges against you?"

"Yes, I have, Your Honor," I replied with an obvious quiver in my voice.

"And are you represented by counsel?"

"Yes, Your Honor. Mr. Weiss." I motioned to him.

"Mr. Weiss, have you discussed the charges with your client?"

"Yes, I have, Your Honor."

"And how does he plead?"

"Innocent of all charges, Your Honor."

"Then let us begin." Judge Harvey motioned for all to take their seats. He was very much in control.

Michael Silva was the assistant district attorney assigned to this case. In his thirties, he appeared to be very young, but he had impressive credentials. He was a Princeton undergraduate who graduated with high honors and then went on to Columbia Law School on scholarship.

"Mr. Silva, I understand you have both physical evidence and corroborating testimony."

"Yes, Your Honor," Mr. Silva stated with obvious confidence.

"And the medical examiner's report? Does that agree with your physical evidence?"

"Well, sir, we don't yet have the medical examiner's report." Small beads of sweat formed on this previously staid prosecutor's forehead. He knew where the judge was going, and it didn't appear that he wanted him to go there.

The judge, who had been perusing the pile of papers in front of him, glanced up at Mr. Silva. "And why is that, Mr. Silva?"

"Well, sir, we do not yet have positive identification of the body."

The room was quiet. The judge sat straight up in his seat. Larry maintained a poker face but grabbed my arm in amazement.

It was the judge who spoke next. "And why not?"

"It appears that the attack and postmortem changes affected the facial features of the victim. A DNA match could not yet be made."

"Excuse me, Mr. Silva? Then on what basis did you originally identify the *deceased* and accuse the defendant?"

"Papers the deceased was carrying, Your Honor, and a watch left near the scene. And motive."

"Did his wife identify him?"

"She has been too distraught, Your Honor, to identify him yet."

"Mr. Silva, I find it disturbing that you accused a man, a well-respected physician, of this violent crime on the limited evidence you describe. How confident are you that the deceased was a victim and that the defendant was the murderer?"

"Very confident, Your Honor."

"And when will we know for sure the identity of the deceased?"

"We are informed that it will only be a very short time until the positive identity is confirmed, Your Honor."

"How long do you expect, Mr. Silva?" Judge Harvey asked with obvious disdain.

"One week. Two at most."

"Then we will convene back here in two weeks. In the interim, Dr. Gifford will be free to return to his normal activities but will be restricted to within twenty miles of his home. Is that agreed, Mr. Weiss?"

"Yes, Your Honor."

"Then two weeks it will be. And Mr. Silva..."

"Yes, Your Honor?"

"We better have positive identification of the deceased at that time." Judge Harvey rose and left the room.

We sat there looking at each other. What just happened?

27

OBFUSCATION

I really did feel good leaving the courthouse. However, something deep down kept me from the elation Larry exhibited.

"Barry, I can't believe our luck. That Ivy Leaguer got caught in his own mess. But we need to find out exactly what he didn't want us to know. Discovery, I call it. He must tell us. It's the law, and he knows it! I'm going to get myself over to his office right now. You OK? You look a little concerned."

"I'm OK. I just can't get away from this feeling that something is just not right."

"Sure, something isn't right. They have the wrong body, or even better, they have the right person, but he died of natural causes."

"Larry, you think that's a real possibility?"

"I've seen many unusual things in this business. It wouldn't be the first time that a person was accused of a crime that didn't even happen."

"How can you be so sure?"

"Well, what I am sure of is that the prosecutor doesn't know who the guy in the morgue really is or even why or how he died. What that means for us is that without evidence, no crime was committed. That, my friend, is a real break!"

"How could they arrest me if they didn't have enough evidence?" I asked with obvious irritation.

"That is what I intend to find out. Maybe he's just inexperienced, or maybe someone he trusted persuaded him. Doesn't really matter for us. If there wasn't a crime committed, he doesn't have a case."

"But what if the body turns out to be Bob's? The medical examiner was just waiting to get some tests back, and what if his report proves murder?"

"Then we'll be back in court fighting. But let me not waste time. I'll find out what's going on and call as soon as I know. Where will you be?"

"I just need time to think. You can reach me on my cell phone."

It seemed so surreal. I was walking but didn't feel the ground. I couldn't hear the cars in the street or the wind whipping between the buildings. All I could feel was the beating of my heart. I had never felt more alone.

My thoughts were random at first: Linda, the children, my practice, and then poor Bob. He was a good person. No harm should have come his way. The watch suddenly popped into my thoughts. I remembered, and it all started making sense.

My wrist had stopped throbbing, but now it was all I could think about. My watch had been switched when I was mugged—that was where it all began. It was at the same time my data was duplicated. This had been a setup from the start. "Damn it!" I blurted out unintentionally. Why was I so naive? All evidence pointed to Dr. Brunswick, but how could I prove it? I didn't even flinch as I bashed my clenched fist against a lone Dumpster and tore skin from my hand. I couldn't believe he would kill for this. I needed to prove his involvement. It was the only way I could reclaim my life. I knew just where to start.

28

PROCUREMENT

Bob and Debra lived in a penthouse on the east side of town. It took almost thirty minutes to get from the courthouse to their neighborhood. That didn't include the time it took to get a cab. It's almost as if you're doing them a favor. I think they only pick up the prospects they know will tip well. I'll never understand how they do that.

The sun was setting as the cab rounded the corner on the way to Bob's apartment. I thought I could find my answer in the papers we had been working on. Prior to his death, we had been working every evening on a presentation to a group of investment bankers. Bob was untiring. He took voluminous notes of our discussions and of the various researchers' presentations and asked an endless array of questions. He had such keen insight and was brilliant to boot. He had returned for graduate training in engineering several years after turning down his medical school acceptances, but he could well pass for a physician with his acquired medical knowledge. We knew it would take more than money to complete the isolation of the substance and begin its synthesis. We needed to find competent researchers who could be trusted. This was one area Bob took very seriously. He took over the recruitment phase, and I couldn't have been happier.

I didn't want to call attention to myself by walking through the lobby and being announced by the doorman. Especially now, after I had been accused of Bob's murder. Bob had given me an extra pass card he had for the elevator in the garage. Conveniently, the garage was around the side of the building. It was a public access garage available to tenants for their own cars—at exorbitant prices, of course.

I entered the garage and walked down the walkway on the side of the ramp. The elevator was located on the lower level to the side of the enclosed booth where the attendant was stationed. The attendant was gone. Two men were talking, standing with their backs to me. I assumed they were waiting for their cars. The lighting was poor, so I could barely make out their shapes in the shadows. Strangely, they were standing in the only darkened area, seemingly intentionally. They were so engrossed in their conversation, they didn't notice me, and I wanted to keep it that way. I had been to the building many times and had met many of Bob's neighbors. All I needed was to have one of them calling the police to say I was there. I ducked into an alcove where I thought I would wait until they got in their car and were on their way. Although I couldn't see them from where I stood, I could overhear their conversation. They were speaking softly.

"You think we'll have time to file?"

"Not sure it really matters. He'll be in jail by tomorrow."

The voices sounded familiar, but too low in volume to identify.

"How can you be so sure?"

"It's all who you know and how much you spend."

A car appeared. The two men entered as the attendant accepted his gratuity. As the car proceeded up the ramp, it passed by the alcove I was hiding in. I poked my head around the wall and was able to clearly see the driver and passenger sitting in the front seat. I was not prepared for what I saw.

It was Bob and Dr. Brunswick!

29

TRANSGRESSIONS

Larry had reached Michael Silva's office, located in an annex of the courthouse, just as he was leaving for the day.

"Mr. Silva, may I have a word with you?"

"This isn't a very good time, Mr. Weiss. Possibly the morning might be a better time?" Silva asked with some uncharacteristic stuttering.

"What do you mean this isn't a good time? It's four in the afternoon. Courts are recessed for the day, and it looks like your office is pretty much deserted."

"OK, five minutes. Only five minutes," he said with newfound courage.

"Look, I don't know what evidence you think you have. But the circumstantial evidence seems transparent. You're prosecuting a reputable doctor who doesn't even have a parking ticket on his record. You don't have a body, and except for a watch that could have been taken from him and switched for a duplicate, no evidence connects him with a crime. So I want to know where you come off saying this isn't a good time and then say I only have five minutes? You have impugned an innocent man's reputation. This is not only a good time, it may well be the only time I give you to disclose your evidence before I file for a dismissal of the charges for lack of evidence and request an investigation of your office's behavior in this affair!"

"Look, Mr. Weiss. I can understand your concern, especially after the hearing today. But I have to tell you the evidence presented to me was quite persuasive."

"What was presented to you? You're a smart guy. What tangible evidence do you have that my client was the murderer? And what would his motive be? You already know that he had kept himself at arm's length from Ludlow's transactions, and in fact, as an employee of the hospital, he didn't stand to profit from any commercial venture. In addition, Bob Ludlow—if that's the body you have in the morgue—was financially sponsoring him and the object of his research. Why in God's name would he kill his cash cow? So unless you have any other evidence that you need to disclose, I would strongly suggest you drop all charges."

Larry was relentless, as he should have been. Small beads of sweat formed on Mr. Silva's brow.

"I can't do that," Mr. Silva stated with an apologetic affect.

"And why not?" Larry bellowed.

"Because this is a lot bigger than you or me," Silva stated, trembling.

"What do you mean by that?" Larry asked incredulously.

"Off the record? You and I are only pawns in a carefully orchestrated game."

With each of Mr. Silva's statements, Larry grew more concerned about the prosecutor's sanity. Mr. Silva's face was pale, he was wringing his hands, and his stuttering speech was obvious. But Larry couldn't stop now. He needed to know what was behind all this. With the prosecutor's obvious weakness—a small crack in the prosecutor's previously impenetrable facade—he saw an opportunity. He had to push hard, and he had to do it now.

"Mr. Silva," he stated authoritatively. "Are you involved in a cover-up? Or do you have information material to this case that you are purposely failing to disclose?"

"I won't. I can't. They'll kill me."

Mr. Silva was now obviously coming apart. Larry stepped toward him, hoping to grab him and possibly return him to his senses. He heard a pop, followed by a whoosh of air next to his ear. Mr. Silva's face was frozen in a horrific grimace. A single hole appeared in his forehead where beads of sweat had glistened. Blood and tissue stained the hallway wall as Mr. Silva's body sank in lifeless cadence to the ground. Larry stood frozen over the body in disbelief of what had just transpired. A coldness overcame him as his knees gave out, and he fell to the floor.

30

AT SEA

I must have been walking for hours yet had no memory of where I had been or even where I was. Just fleeting thoughts. Pieces of disconnected images strung together in random fashion. I was not in control, and this frightened me. If Bob was alive, why hadn't he contacted me? He obviously knew I was being accused of his murder. Didn't he care? I thought we were friends. And why was he with Dr. Brunswick? I kept trying to think of reasons that would explain what I had witnessed and exculpate Bob from involvement in what appeared to be his betrayal of our friendship. However, none were forthcoming, and the obvious made me furious.

I needed to clear my head and try to make sense of what was happening. I couldn't yet tell Linda what I saw. I wasn't even sure what I did see. All I knew was Dr. Brunswick and Bob Ludlow were in the car together and talking. And Bob was alive! Then who was dead? At least I couldn't be accused of his murder.

Anytime I had to think things out, I was always drawn to the sea. I hadn't been to my boat in weeks. I hailed a cab. It was almost time to take it out of the water for the winter. The weather was unpredictable. However, today the sky was clear, the winds blowing lightly from the north. The sun was just above the horizon, greeting the sea with its calming glow.

It was great having the boat. When I first started my practice, I would often try to sneak away from my office during lunch and drive the ten minutes to the boat, just to eat a sandwich for a few minutes and then force myself to drive back. But for those few minutes, I felt as if I were on holiday. I always felt calm when I was on the water. The sights and smells and gentle rocking of the ship would put me to sleep, if I allowed. But this time I needed to have a little time to think things over. I just hoped that its magic would work.

As expected for this late in the season, the marina parking was empty. Only two cars were there. I recognized one as belonging to Jen, a capable teenager who lucked out having a job as the lifeguard at the marina's pool. During the season, it was busy on the weekends, but during the week, it was usually empty. Most of the time you could find Jen curled up with a good book, or so you thought. More often she would be catching up on sleep from the prior evening's partying. However, now the pool was closed, and she used the solitude of the place for studying. The other car, a nondescript black Caprice with darkened windows, was new to me. It didn't have a marina decal on its fender, so I thought it must be a friend of Jen's.

I parked away from these vehicles, mirroring my need for seclusion. I loved the walk down the dock to the boat. It was the transition between the stresses of work and the serenity of leisure. The marina was a small private facility with few amenities, but it did have a pool, a grassy area for picnics, and dockage for about thirty boats ranging in size from twenty to fifty feet. My boat was average size for the marina at thirty-five feet. It had twin inboard gasoline engines. After fifteen years, the ravages of time had yellowed the fiberglass, and it required increasingly more work for me to keep up with the brightwork. But it was my love of this vessel and the solace it gave me that enjoined me to spend countless weekends during the winter in its employ. But it was mine. I bought it from a colleague who relocated out west several years ago. He never really used it or took care of it, so I got it for a song. But it needed so much work that I kept pouring money into it. Fortunately, I was able to do a lot of the work myself. It was great therapy.

I thought I'd head out to the Sandpit, a small cove off the sound about a half hour's ride. Being early in the day, I'd have a good four to five hours before the tide ebbed and the entrance to the small cove narrowed, making egress difficult. It would be a good place to drop anchor and just be able to think. I never had the time to get out on the water during the week. I was sure the Sandpit would be empty.

I freed some of the lines and prepared the boat for voyage. I always checked the oil, water, and transmission levels prior to taking out the boat. An old but important habit I learned from my dad. The engines started up with their usual ardor. It was a sound that was both calming and exciting. I freed the remaining lines and began my voyage. The waters were calm. Pulling away from the dock, I began to feel my head clearing.

I don't know why, but I felt I was being watched. I looked around and couldn't see anyone. I could see that the same cars were in the parking lot at the marina. I saw the driver's door close on the black Caprice.

I glanced back as I moved farther away from the dock. *Odd,* I thought. The black Caprice seemed to be inching forward instead of backing out of the spot, as if to get a better look at me. I wondered why they didn't get out of the car. The day was beautiful.

As I rounded Shippan Point, which was less than a quarter mile from the dock, I noticed an unusual smell. It smelled like burned rubber, like the garbage plant five miles away might be burning refuse. However, I saw no smoke in front of me, and it seemed to be coming from my boat! I looked toward the exhausts and saw white smoke. It could mean water or possibly oil. Almost as soon as I saw it, an alarm started screeching. This couldn't be good. Black smoke was now emanating from the transom. The cabin was filling with black acrid smoke. A glance at the gauges showed the engine was redlining. I had to shut it down before it ignited the fuel. I shut off the circuit breaker, but still it continued. I feared it was not long before the boat would be in flames. I called a Mayday on the radio as I grabbed my life jacket. The coast guard answered as I saw the first flames coming from the engine room. I gave them my location and headed forward to drop the anchor and get as far from the fire as possible. I couldn't make it to the life raft on the bridge over the engine room.

The fire was engulfing the boat. I had to get off. I hoped the coast guard was nearby. I stood on the bow, readying myself to jump. I heard a thundering noise from behind. The force of the explosion was enormous. The last thing I remembered was being hurled forward from the bow.

31

COVER-UP

"This is out of control," Larry blurted, bouncing off the stairway walls and finally exiting the building through the front door. He ran into a cop patrolling the street in front of the courthouse. He pointed his finger at the office building where the assistant district attorney lay on the floor, blood staining the carpet.

"He's…been…shot. I think he's dead!" he screamed as he stuttered his way through the words.

"Whoa, buddy. Who's been shot and where?" the patrolman calmly questioned.

"Michael Silva, the assistant district attorney. I was just talking with him in the hallway outside his office, and then a shot out of nowhere hit him, and he fell to the floor." Larry's voice was tight as he fought to catch his breath.

"What's the office number and approximate time of the shooting?" the cop responded, clearly focused as he made a call on his radio. "Officer Brighton, Badge 5234, at Six Courthouse Street."

"Just minutes ago. Suite two-nineteen," Larry responded.

"Shots fired, victim injured, unknown assailant. Need SWAT and EMS now," the cop continued.

"Your location?" the dispatcher asked.

"Outside the building at the intersection of Court and Waters," Officer Brighton replied.

"You're requested to prevent entrance to the building and retain any persons exiting until backup arrives. ETA two minutes," the dispatcher's crackling voice ordered.

"Roger," Officer Brighton responded. "Your name, sir?" He directed Larry to walk with him toward the entrance of the building.

"Larry Weiss, I'm an attorney with Weiss, Cottler, and Spivack."

"Mr. Weiss, please stay here until my supervisor arrives," Officer Brighton ordered as he finished writing the name in his notebook and then began blocking the entrance and detaining all persons exiting the building.

Approximately fifteen persons were detained on the grassy lawn outside the courthouse as SWAT and EMS arrived almost at the same time. Less than five minutes had transpired since the radio call was made. SWAT took up position around the building and at rooftops across the street. Others led the workers on the grass to a SWAT vehicle for interrogation. Three entered the building, fully armed. They made their way to the second floor up the stairs.

"Clear," one SWAT team member exclaimed.

"Clear," another said.

"All clear," echoed each in sequence.

"Where the hell's the body?" the sergeant asked with obvious irritation. His heart was still pumping with the high of the moment.

"He did say suite two-nineteen, didn't he?"

"Yes, Sarge."

"And what is that smell? Cleaning fluid?"

"Sure does smell like it."

"OK, guys, let's check the building. Tim, you check the upper floors. Bill, the lower floors. Keep the mics open. I don't think we're going to find anything. I think it's a wild-goose chase. Someone has a lot of answering to do."

The sergeant checked the floor while waiting for the response from his men. Neither found anything on the upper or lower floors.

He walked down the hallway to a window at the end. *Great view of the area,* he thought.

A grocery delivery van turned slowly around the corner down Court Street. *Odd to be delivering groceries in a business district,* he thought. In a moment, he was on the radio to other agents outside. "Grocery van just turned left on Court Street. Stop it, and check it out. Proceed with extreme caution."

In moments, sirens were wailing, and patrol cars were in hot pursuit. At first, the grocery van made no attempt to escape until several patrol cars approached. Then all hell broke loose. The van raced down the main street at speeds exceeding eighty miles per hour, missing pedestrians and other vehicles by inches. The occupants of the van made no attempt to fire on the officers. It appeared they had this all planned: head down Court Street to Chambers and onto the highway. At the entrance to the highway, they rammed a car, setting it ablaze and effectively blocking entrance to the highway. They had to have known that the right-hand lanes were under construction and that workers weren't there at this time. They broke through the barricades and careened down the shoulder, getting off at the exit to the tunnel. The patrol cars were blocked from pursuing them, and the choppers wouldn't be able to track them through the tunnel. The van was found abandoned in the tunnel. They must have changed cars in the tunnel. They knew what they were doing.

Larry waited nervously near the building. He had heard the commotion and was only a few yards from the SWAT van when it took off after the delivery van. He had no idea why the chase ensued and what might have been inside the delivery van until a well-dressed man with a detective badge hanging from his pocket approached him.

"Are you Mr. Weiss?"

"Yes, I am," Larry answered a bit brusquely.

"I'm Detective O'Brien of homicide. I understand you've been through a bit of a scare."

"Bit of a scare? A man was killed right in front of me!" He couldn't believe the insensitivity of the detective.

"Well, that's where we have a problem. You see, no body was found."

"What? He was killed right in front of me. A body just doesn't disappear, does it?"

"No, it doesn't. Why don't you come inside with me and show me what happened, so we can figure this out," Detective O'Brien responded.

"Thank you, absolutely."

With that, the detective and Larry walked inside the building. They took the elevator up to the second floor. Larry would have walked the stairs, but Detective O'Brien had an old knee injury from his football days and experienced pain when climbing stairs.

They reached the hallway in front of suite 219. There was no body, no blood, and no evidence of a shot being fired. Just the smell of cleaning fluid in the air.

"This where your buddy was shot?" Detective O'Brien asked.

"He wasn't my buddy, but this was certainly the place," Larry said.

Was he hallucinating? He did see Mr. Silva shot right here. But where was the corpse? This was getting stranger by the minute.

32

BAD TIMES

"No! No! Get away from me!" I blurted, not knowing I was lying in the marsh by the shoreline with the willows tickling my neck. I was waking up. My head hurt, and I had that metallic taste you get when your gums are bleeding. My memory of the explosion soon returned. If it weren't for my life jacket, I probably would have ended up like the pieces of fiberglass and shredded life jackets currently buffeting the shoreline. I had floated back toward the marina after the explosion.

It was getting dark. It must have been hours since the explosion. I was surprised not to find the area crawling with would-be rescuers. Possibly my call to the coast guard hadn't gone through. The radio might have even been sabotaged. Even though the marina was in a secluded cove, someone must have heard the explosion. A chill came over me. I had to get away from here. If help didn't come, then they would at least want to see if I was dead—or finish the job.

I pulled my way up the embankment. My hands had difficulty closing, my body was aching, but I knew I couldn't afford to rest. I had to get back home and get Linda to a safe place. I was convinced they would not stop until I was dead. I reached the high grass and rolled on my back to remove my life jacket. I heard voices in the distance. I couldn't quite make out what they were saying, but they sounded angry. I had to somehow get back to my car. I felt in my pockets and was relieved to find my keys where I had left them. I didn't want to be seen or heard since I didn't know who belonged to the voices. I crawled on my belly for what seemed like forever until I was at the edge of the parking lot. A sea breeze was blowing the trees, covering the sound of my movements. The black Caprice was gone. I quickly pulled myself up and made a dash for my car. I hesitated before starting it, thinking the worst. Fortunately, it started without event. I drove out of the lot and didn't look back.

I wasn't followed.

They must think I'm dead. Why else would the Caprice be gone, and why weren't they looking for me on the banks of the channel? This might be a good thing, I thought. *I might be able to turn the tables on them if they think I'm dead.*

I still needed to let Linda know I was all right and contact Larry to let him know what had happened and what I saw. I also wanted to know how his negotiating was going with the assistant district attorney. But how was I going to speak with them without giving myself away? This was going to be difficult.

I entered my office through the back entrance. I thought this would be the last place they would look for me. My cell phone was soaked and dead. I left my work cell phone in my desk, and hopefully it was still there. I needed to let people know I was alive. I did some first aid on myself in the bathroom and then called Larry on his cell phone. It was best to call and not attempt to see him in person. I also didn't think they, whoever "they" were, had the wherewithal to intercept cell phone conversations. I wasn't that paranoid…yet. Larry answered on the first ring.

"Jesus, Barry, where have you been? I've been trying to reach you all day, and you can imagine how crazy Linda has been."

"Look, I know, but I had to get away. Too many things were happening too quickly. I saw Bob alive."

"Bob Ludlow alive? What are you talking about? Where?"

"Well, when I left you at the courthouse, I went to Bob's apartment building, hoping to find some notes or papers in his apartment that would explain what was going on," I started to explain.

"That was a dumb thing to do. They could have arrested you for breaking and entering and thrown you in jail," Larry scolded me.

"Listen, I didn't even get to his apartment. I entered through the garage, hoping not to be seen, and that's where I saw Dr. Brunswick and Bob in a car together talking like good ol' buddies. I couldn't believe it. I needed to get away to make sense of this. I didn't think I was followed. I went to my boat and started out into the bay. A fire started; fortunately I had my life jacket on when the boat exploded and threw me into the bay. I was unconscious and drifted toward shore. I finally awoke and crawled ashore. Larry...they're trying to kill me, and I'm not even sure why!"

"You have any proof it was Bob you saw in the car with Dr. Brunswick?" Larry asked in his usual adversarial way.

"Only my eyes and ears. What do you think? I took a camera and tape recorder with me?" I thought I'd better change the subject before I lost it. "You have any luck with the assistant district attorney?"

"Yeah, great luck. He was shot right in front of me!"

"What! You can't be serious," I said incredulously.

"I sure am. But what's even weirder, I ran to get help, and when the cops arrived, the body was gone. Fortunately, they chased a van leaving the scene, which of course they lost. They probably would have thrown me in jail for filing a false report!"

"Larry, what's going on?"

"I'm not sure, but I have a feeling this is a lot bigger than we ever imagined."

"Listen, Larry. I need you to get in touch with Linda and tell her I'm all right. Best if you don't say anything about you speaking with me. At least for now. Try not to alarm her, but see if she'll go to her mom's for at least a week. I'll contact her there."

"Why don't you call her?"

"I can't. They must not know I'm still alive. It's my only chance."

"OK, I'll call her now. When will I hear from you?"

"I'll give you a call tomorrow around nine o'clock in the morning. Be careful," I cautioned.

"You too," he echoed.

Larry hung up. I heard a second click a moment later.

33

REPROMED

I knew where I was going. How did I know? It made sense. It felt right. I needed to know if what I saw in the garage was what it seemed. There was a lingering suspicion I had about the motivation of ReproMed in gifting the sequencer. Why would an unknown entity spend so much to support research from a potential competitor? There was also something that concerned me about Bob's involvement with this company, having seen Bob and Brunswick together in the garage. Not yet sure what it was. But I felt ReproMed was where all the answers would be found. I was sure of it. I knew that I was taking a risk calling, but I had no alternative.

To get through the security would not be simple, though. I needed to be persuasive—very persuasive. I first called to speak with Matt Dean, one of the technical folks I had met with previously. The operator connected me to his secretary after asking me to hold for a moment.

"Matt Dean speaking."

"Matt, good morning. It's Barry Gifford."

I didn't know if he had heard about the report of Bob's death, and I didn't want to bring it up. I wasn't sure they would speak with me if Bob were no longer in the negotiations, even though the terms of the agreement with Bob gave either of us sole ownership if the other were incapacitated. I needed to talk with the principals of the firm to find out who was involved in the deal and who had the most to gain or lose. That's where the answer would lie.

"Hey, Barry, how are you? Haven't spoken to you in a while. Horrible thing that happened to Bob. Did they find his murderer?" Matt asked.

Well, it was obvious he knew Bob was killed, but it didn't seem he knew that I had been accused of his murder. That gave me the opening I needed. "No, they haven't. They've gotten a few leads but nothing definite. It's a huge loss for all of us."

"We all were hoping you would call. In fact, if I didn't hear from you, I was supposed to give you a call. We're very interested in concluding the deal for Tesbloc. The annual stockholders' meeting is in a few weeks, and we'd like to present Tesbloc at the meeting. That means we need to get it to the attorneys soon. I know it's a trying time for you, but as soon as you feel up to it, we should set up a meeting."

Unbelievable. I couldn't have arranged it better. "That's why I'm calling. I really need to keep myself busy. I thought I might try to keep involved and keep my mind off this tragedy. I certainly would like to talk with the group Bob had been dealing with."

"Well, you couldn't have called at a better time. All the partners are in conference this morning. Later this morning would be a great time to speak with them. If you would like, I'll arrange to put you on the agenda," Matt offered graciously.

"Sounds great! What time would you like me there?"

"Why don't you meet me at ten o'clock at my office?"

"I'll be there."

I hung up the phone and thought about what had just transpired. They knew about Bob and still wanted to see me. They were also under a time constraint to conclude the deal. It seemed too good to be true.

I needed to clean up. I couldn't go into a meeting looking like this, and I couldn't go home. I felt the best place to go was my racquetball club. I always kept a fresh change of clothes there.

It was just before 10:00 a.m. when I approached the building, a twenty-five-story monolithic structure in the downtown area. A security guard was at the front desk. I had been to the building a few times with Bob during the early negotiations of Tesbloc. I never got to meet the principals, just the technical people like Matt. I guess I felt it was odd at the time that those investing so heavily in the project wouldn't insist on meeting with me, but maybe all they really cared about was Tesbloc's potential as a moneymaker, and for that they had the insight of one of their own kind—Bob Ludlow.

I was escorted to Matt's office on the tenth floor. His secretary apologized for his absence. He had been called into the same meeting I was to join. She stated that he had left instructions for her to escort me to the anteroom just outside the boardroom.

I was asked to wait in a beautiful cherry-wood-paneled room with portraits of the founders adorning the walls. I looked at each of the four portraits with admiration for the artist—such depth of color and a truly remarkable ability to portray personality with facial expression. It was at the last portrait when my face paled and knees quivered. It was an evil-looking man, fortyish, with deep-set piercing blue eyes. The face was well chiseled with black hair gelled back. The plaque underneath read DEXTER L. BRUNSWICK, MD, PRESIDENT, 1992–PRESENT.

34

THE BOARDROOM

I was still nonplussed when the huge mahogany doors to the conference room opened. Only the thunderous noise of the doors closing against each other returned me to the moment. And there, seated at a large table desk, like a judge's bench, were three men: Dr. Brunswick, Bob Ludlow, and a third man who looked familiar, but whom I didn't recognize. There were also two muscular men who quickly patted me down for weapons and grabbed my arms as if they were nonliving tissue and forced me into a chair in front of the table.

"Welcome, Dr. Gifford," Dr. Brunswick said with obvious gloating.

"What the hell is going on?" I responded. My heart continued pounding.

"Did you have a rough day?" Dr. Brunswick responded almost mockingly.

I looked directly at Bob, hoping for an expression of warmth, a glimmer of compassion. "Bob, I can't believe you are part of this," I said, not wanting it to be true.

Bob was looking in my direction but not at me. It appeared he wanted to reply but Brunswick responded instead.

"Dr. Gifford," Dr. Brunswick responded. "There are many things you know as truths that are based only loosely on reality. Take for instance, your patient, your friend, Bob. To you, he was a victim of malfeasance, or is he now part of this dark plot? You're not quite sure, are you?"

I really wasn't sure of anything right now. I still couldn't believe Bob had a part to play in all this. His gaze did not change. In fact, his body showed no movement at all except for his breathing, which became more rapid. Was he drugged?

"Let me tell you a story," Dr. Brunswick began. "It's about triplets, male triplets, born to a very wealthy man—a businessman, a financial genius, and a hunter of unusual prowess. He would travel the globe in search of the perfect game. He was a man's man, quick with decisions and intolerant of anyone or anything that didn't meet his standards. Why, he fired a cook who had worked for him for ten years for just burning his toast and an entire division of his company when they failed to meet quarterly projections for their first time ever. He also had an intolerance for imperfection. Imperfection in material possessions, and imperfection in people. He was a bigoted man.

"The mother of the triplets, his wife, died in childbirth. Infection, they said at the time. Two of the babies did not meet his standards, and these two imperfect babies were quickly given up for adoption. He kept the child who appeared normal and sent the two who were not to an orphanage. The father had not thought of these two imperfect children as living, breathing wonders of life. These children did nothing wrong, other than being born. He remarried soon after the death of his first wife. But even this wife didn't know about the triplets. She was never told that more than a single child had been born."

Dr. Brunswick continued, and his voice grew louder. "This man could not tolerate imperfection." A perceptible stutter came to his voice. "In one of these two discarded babies, the sex could not be determined—not exactly a boy and not exactly a girl. *Ambiguous* was the term they used. An inborn error, a cruel joke by mother nature. Because of the lack of development of the external sex organs, the doctors had recommended surgery to change that little boy to a little girl. They said it would be better that way. The child would be able to fit in with society, they said. This man, this hunter, would not hear of it. No son of his would be changed to a girl. He could not cope with this imperfection. The little baby was unwanted. Thrown out like garbage," he stated emphatically.

The room was quiet as he extended his mad tirade. Bob still did not move. His muscles were paralyzed.

"The other rejected baby was sickly," he continued. "Barely surviving childbirth and not given much hope for life. Again, he could not deal with this imperfection. He did not know that this child would survive and grow up to be a doctor with two children of his own."

He looked directly at me while saying this. Who was the other abandoned child? Did he think it was me? Who was the other orphaned baby? The answer was not long in coming.

His impassioned diatribe appeared to be his catharsis. He recovered his composure and again looked directly at me. His rage was rekindled. "That was then, and this is now. It was, in a way, God's payback; the child he kept, the only one he loved and was devoted to, had a dark secret. All that was missing from the discarded son was present in the revered son. If he only knew that this son was also imperfect. I wonder what he would have done. He never told his son that he had other siblings. The son with ambiguous genitalia grew up in an orphanage until the age of eighteen. He was then the age of majority and could decide where he would live. Growing up, he was continuously abused by the other children in the orphanage without intervention by the director or the staff. He was left beaten and bloodied. He was a small child without defenses. He was also without the support and protection a family provides. Without a mother who's there in the middle of the night when you have a nightmare, and without the father you go to a ball game with and want and need as a role model. The other rejected son overcame his illness and was adopted as an infant. Never to be heard of again. Until a chance meeting."

Dr. Brunswick continued with his venomous rant. "The boy who remained in the orphanage spent much time in search of his roots. They were difficult to trace. He uncovered a second ill baby who was delivered to the same orphanage about the same time he was. This baby was adopted shortly after arriving. He also discovered that the man who dropped him off at the orphanage was wealthy and had a son. It would be about thirty years before the separated sons would meet—and a chance meeting at that—one as a patient and one as a doctor. The doctor knew almost immediately that this was a very special patient. He didn't realize how special a patient until a DNA match confirmed that he and the patient were a genetic match. They were siblings and had just found each other. Three babies born, two with inborn errors, and one perfectly normal whose genome held the key to eliminating fertility in those who had their amusement at my expense. I will get even, and you will help me, brother," he stated to my utter amazement.

He thinks I'm his brother! How the hell does he think that?

He continued, "You were the other brother discarded by our father and sent to the orphanage after your birth on September 16, 1955. You will help me change the world."

He was obviously delusional. I had no idea why he thought I was his brother and sent to the orphanage. Help him change the world? Was he also insane? Either he knew something about me that I didn't, or he was having a psychotic break. Nonetheless, I needed to get out of here and get help. No matter what it was, I was not going to be part of his twisted vision of the future.

Brunswick nodded to one of his goons. I was grabbed from behind. A hood was placed over my head. A sweet odor penetrated my sinuses. I felt dizzy.

35

THE PRISONER

Was I in heaven…or hell? What time was it? What day was it? There were no lights in the room. No sounds at all. I was on my back, my feet dangling off the bed. It was cold and hard. No covers, just a mattress. A damp smell was in the air. I was starting to wake from the drug-induced fog. The room seemed like it was spinning, and I found it difficult to move. I felt sick to my stomach, and my head was ready to explode. I had felt this way before.

I worried about my family. They were in great danger. Brunswick would stop at nothing to get out of me what he needed. I wouldn't let him win. I felt the fire rekindled and growing inside me. I also knew he couldn't let me live, knowing what I knew. He would dispose of me quickly once he had his prize. He would threaten my family to control me. I needed to get out of here to warn them—to protect them.

But how was I to escape? I didn't even know where I was, and I couldn't see my surroundings. The last thing I remembered was one of the goons grabbing me and placing a hood over my head. I really didn't remember much more. Bob was alive. That meant I couldn't, or shouldn't, be accused of his murder. Bob and Dr. Brunswick were siblings, and they thought I was too. I couldn't believe that! Those two were as different as two people could be. Bob was an altruistic introvert who preferred to be behind the scenes. Dexter Brunswick, on the other hand, was ruthless and greedy and needed to be the center of attention. What was I missing? Why the charade? They knew that Bob couldn't feign being dead for too long. Someone was bound to recognize him. There was another option, but it just seemed too complex to carry out. What if everything had been staged—the arrest, the lockup, the court case—all to keep me from disclosing the secrets only I knew?

How could they do it? The detective at the house holding me overnight in jail. The courtroom and judge. No, it was too elaborate. It required too much involvement from too many people. They could have faked a murder and accused me of the crime. But there was a body. Whose body was it? My head was still hurting. It was hard for me to think. All I wanted to do was sleep. I heard footsteps outside the room and then keys in the lock. A tall muscular figure entered. I couldn't make out any facial features since the light was projecting from behind him. He clicked a wall switch. Suddenly, the room was ablaze. My eyes closed in response to the insult.

"Come with me," he said with an obvious Swedish accent.

"Where are you taking me?" My eyes were still mostly closed.

He didn't respond. He just grabbed my arm with an almost vise-like grip.

"Hey, buddy? Could you go a little easier on your grip?" I said as my arm became numb from the pain. He didn't answer.

We entered a darkened passageway. It appeared that we were underground. No windows in sight. The lack of sound was eerie, and there was a dank smell. As my eyes adapted to the light, I could see another door in the distance and my escort's semiautomatic Glock. I had no doubt he knew how to use it. He probably didn't know that I did too. The Glock was very reliable. It almost never misfired. Squeeze the trigger and the magazine fired ten rounds. The safety was incorporated into the trigger mechanism. This goon carried it on his waist on the left side in an unlatched holster—a very unconventional way that made it very accessible to me. When I was face-to-face with him, I could easily extend my right hand and take it from him. If only the opportunity presented itself. If only I could gather the courage.

I also had no way of knowing whether the gun was loaded, and the bullet was chambered. I knew if I did grab it, I would have only a split-second until he would try to regain possession and either shoot or pistol-whip me. I would have to fire the gun at point-blank range and exit quickly before the others arrived.

It all happened so quickly. I heard a bloodcurdling scream of fear echo up the passageway, followed by the explosive crackle of a gun being fired. It sounded like an execution. And I was headed in that direction. If I were to make my move, it had to be now. We passed a ladder attached to the wall of the passageway that led upward. *An escape route,* I thought. Given the distance to the room where the shots were fired, I thought I'd have at least twenty seconds before I would have to be out of sight.

I stopped short. The blond Swede turned toward me as I had expected. He still maintained a grip on my left arm. With my right arm free, I grabbed for his gun. It released freely into my hand. I brought it up to his abdomen and could feel his abdominal muscles pushing at the barrel. I pulled the trigger. A muffled explosion followed. The grip on my left arm loosened and then released as the muscular Swede fell to the floor. I bolted to the ladder and started climbing, hoping that my freedom would be found above.

36

THE CONSPIRACY

It seemed to take an eternity to climb the ladder. I climbed as fast as I could. My fingers were raw from the cold steel and rough walls. I had thought I was still in the city, either underground or in an abandoned tunnel. However, I could be anywhere. At the top of the ladder, I squeezed through a crevice and exited my prison at the bottom of a hill. I scaled up the hill and then slid down the other side it into the moonlit night. I picked myself up and kept on running. I knew what was behind me. The smell of pine needles filled the air. The night was serene. I kept on running through the trees, through a field, and then onto a dirt road. I wasn't sure what direction I should go. The wrong choice might lead back to my captors.

The road curved sharply ahead. I could see headlights. They were coming my way. I jumped into the ground cover off to the side of the road just as an older-model pickup truck appeared around the curve. It was moving slowly. Were they after me? I couldn't be sure. Would they see me with their lights as they came closer? I was petrified. Then I heard music. I dared raise my head from the dirt as they closed in on my position. I could make out the silhouette of a woman holding a baby in the passenger seat, and the driver was a man with a large hat. *A family, certainly not a threat,* I thought. I could get a ride out of this place. I waited until they passed my hiding place to make my move. I bolted to my feet and ran to the back of the moving truck.

With one quick jump, I was on the truck. I covered myself with an old piece of burlap. Their music continued to play.

I rode for the better part of the night in the back of the pickup. I tried to make a mental map of our course. It was difficult to concentrate. I was so tired that I could hardly keep my eyes open. I found myself drifting off to sleep. Only the potholes in the road jolted me awake.

The sun rose above a darkened city. We were approaching from the west. As the light of day appeared, I was able to see a little more of my surroundings. The burlap I was hiding under was also covering file boxes that looked very familiar. I needed a little more light to see them, so I lifted the burlap a bit. The boxes were stamped with consecutive numbers. I was able to make out the name printed on the box: R-E-P-R-O-M-E-D. I could not believe what I was reading. Whose truck was this, and where were we heading? I needed to get a look in the box to see what was in there.

I opened the box nearest to me. The box was filled with files labeled "Tesbloc clinical studies—Phase I." Tesbloc clinical studies? We had only used animals for the initial studies. We weren't ready for human trials yet. The animal studies clearly had problems. It would be unethical and dangerous to even attempt studies in humans. What was going on here? I kept reading. "Patient #02–216 exhibited a failure of spermatogenesis at thirty-six days after a single dose. Accompanied by side effects of hypertension and headaches. MRI demonstrates cerebral bleed, primarily occipital." Those bastards! They were using patients as guinea pigs. Where did they get these "patients," and how did they explain the complications when they required hospitalization?

Things began making sense. I knew what happened to these patients—I had just witnessed the "retiring" of one last evening. But why was Bob involved? I still couldn't figure this out. I kept searching in the other boxes and kept finding even more disturbing data. I wondered if there was any documentation in these boxes that would clear me of the murder charges. In the third box, I found my papers on Tesbloc. How did they get these? Only a few trusted individuals had access to this data—and Bob was one. I also found a file folder labeled "Barry Gifford." Inside was a single lab chromosome report that I had ordered on many of my infertility patients. It concluded, "Normal male 46XY, intact Y chromosome positive for a NR5A1 mutation." This confirmed my suspicion that they had sampled my blood in the parking lot. I wasn't sure about the significance of the NR5A1 mutation, but it was likely the reason Brunswick thought I was his brother.

I quickly put the papers back as the truck pulled up to a diner and stopped. The driver and passenger got out. They walked past the back of the truck on their way into the restaurant. The burly man was tightly holding on to the woman. It didn't appear that the woman was a willing participant. However, I could clearly see her kissing and holding the baby tightly. *So much in love with this precious child,* I thought, which was in stark contrast to the roughness of her companion. The woman turned her head back toward me as she repositioned the baby on her shoulder. I was shocked! It was Debra Ludlow. With a baby! I know they had not yet proceeded with in vitro fertilization. I had to speak with her. I got the feeling that the driver was one of Dr. Brunswick's henchmen. If he left her alone, even for a moment, I would have the opportunity.

I saw them enter the diner. I made my move quickly. I exited the back of the pickup truck, making sure everything was back in order. My opportunity was soon in coming as Debra's companion made his way to the restroom. I quickly entered the diner and slid next to Debra in the booth. I knew I had precious few moments.

I covered Debra's mouth with my hand, so she wouldn't scream when I surprised her with my appearance. "Debra, it's me, Barry. Please be calm." I was right. She was surprised to see me. I was glad I covered her mouth to muffle her scream.

"Barry, you're alive. They told me you had died in a boating accident."

"They tried, Debra. They tried real hard but have not yet succeeded. I need to know what's going on. I don't have much time."

"Meet me outside the ladies' room when he comes back to the table," she said.

I didn't know whether to trust her. But I had to. I had no alternative. "I will. Just please don't take too long. I'm worried about your safety—and mine." I moved to another part of the restaurant. I made sure I'd have access to the exit. Just in case.

Her companion returned to the table, and as she said she would, she went with the baby to the restroom. I met her in the vestibule by the phone.

"Debra, tell me why I'm being framed for Bob's murder when he's alive. And whose baby is this?"

"The baby is mine or soon will be. Dr. Brunswick arranged for a private adoption. The baby was an orphan. The mother mysteriously died in childbirth, and the father could not be found. The baby was put up for adoption. But what do you mean about being framed for Bob's murder? Bob's not dead! I just left him. Why would anyone make up such a story?"

I believed Debra. I needed to know what Bob's involvement was. "Debra, what did Bob tell you?"

"He only said that the baby had no relatives and that we were the only people who could take care of the little one. He also said he needed to speak with Dr. Brunswick about a project they had been working on. I thought he hated Dr. Brunswick for all he had done to him. I never thought he would ever have dealings with him."

"Who's the guy with you?" I asked.

"Bob said he would take me back home and protect me. He scares me. He grabs my arm so tight I want to scream with pain. I just want to protect the baby. You know how much we wanted a child. Maybe we will be successful with IVF, but this opportunity presented to us, and we just could not pass it up. It's a dream come true. Too bad it had to come from such an unfortunate situation."

An unfortunate situation, for sure. I wondered how Dr. Brunswick had arranged the mother's death during childbirth. Nonetheless, I understood how Debra felt. Many of my patients felt the same way. They had been trying to conceive for so long, and if a situation presented itself, they would jump at the opportunity. I still didn't know about the depth of Bob's involvement with ReproMed, but I knew we were talking for too long. "Debra, you better get back to the table before you're missed. I'll contact you at home. Please don't say anything about our meeting to anyone, even Bob, until I get this all sorted out. Will you do that for me?"

"Barry, I'll do my best. You know I never keep anything from Bob."

"I know I'm asking a lot, but many lives are at stake."

"Barry, will you be all right?"

"I hope so, Debra. I'm really concerned about my family right now."

Whatever was going on, it sure didn't seem like Debra was in on it. Linda must be going crazy not having heard from me. She probably thought I was dead. I almost was—several times. I could not shake myself of this sense of impending tragedy. I was not used to this feeling. They were surely looking for me. There was only one way they could control me. A sickening feeling enveloped me. I had to find Linda before they did.

37

ABDUCTION

Linda was up at 4:00 a.m. after very little sleep. She had been kept late at the police station and then toured all the hospitals in town to look for Barry. She had left Justin and Diana with her mother-in-law. After only three hours of sleep, she was going to start again to find out where her husband was or what might have happened to him. It had been forty-eight hours since her husband had left the courthouse, but it seemed like weeks. She knew something was terribly wrong when he didn't call after the hearing. She had heard from Larry. He told her that Barry needed some time alone to think things through. This wasn't like him, but this situation was like nothing he had ever experienced. Larry had not heard from him since.

Linda entered the police station and proceeded to the sergeant's desk.

"Good morning, Mrs. Gifford." Sergeant Dines greeted her with his usual jovial disposition. Sergeant Dines was a man in his late fifties who had been placed on desk duty after he froze in a hostage situation.

"I wish it was a better morning, Sergeant. Any word about my husband?"

"Nothing yet, ma'am. We'll certainly contact you if we hear anything."

A Detective and a female officer overhearing the conversation walked up to the desk and asked, "Mrs. Gifford, my partner and I are helping with the investigation. We were just about to call you. Would you have a moment to speak to us?"

"Certainly. Have you found my husband?"

"Not yet. I just want to ask you a few questions to help with the investigation." They proceeded to a conference room not far from the sergeant's desk. "Mrs. Gifford," the detective said after he closed the door. "Have any funds been taken from your joint account?"

"That's a curious question. Why do you ask?" Linda didn't know what to make of the question.

"Well, it has been our experience that when a person on bail disappears, he might have been motivated to seek a more protected environment."

"If you're implying that my husband is trying to jump bail, you're dead wrong. He's an honorable man who is innocent of the charges against him." Linda was livid and not hiding her anger. "He is, and has been, an upstanding leader in our community, and besides, he has two beautiful children he adores. There's no way he would run!"

"I just bring it up as a possibility. Nothing more. Please check your bank accounts, and let me know if anything unusual has occurred."

Linda was on the verge of losing it. She had to get out of there quickly. She didn't know where to start. Her cell phone rang as she approached her car.

"Hello," she answered. No response from the other end. Just a quiet hush. She thought she could almost make out someone breathing. It was a muffled sound. She recognized the number on the screen—her mother-in-law's. "Justin, Diana, is that you?" Her anxiety continued to grow when no answer was forthcoming.

Thinking that her mother-in-law might be hurt, she asked, "Mom, is everything all right?" She raised her voice as if to project it further into the room on the other end. Then she heard the sound no mother wants to hear: the cry of unbridled fear from her child. "Diana, what's the matter? Please answer me! Oh my God, please answer."

Tears clouded her vision. She could hear the pounding of her heart and feel her throat tightening. She was about to close the phone when a male voice stated, “If you want to see your children alive, be at this house within twenty minutes. If you inform anyone, your kids die.” Before she could utter a word, the connection went dead.

38

CRISIS

Helicopters circled overhead. A two-mile perimeter was in place. Vehicle searches were being conducted of anyone leaving or entering the area. A child had been shot, point-blank, execution-style, the news reports stated. A radical group was claiming responsibility. The reports stated it was meant as a warning to his father. A warning! For God's sake, they killed a child! How could anyone have so much hatred? Children were supposed to remain innocent and not become pawns in a political power struggle. Was there no sanity in this world? Barry couldn't listen to this anymore. He walked past the televisions on display toward the exit doors.

Sunrise was still an hour away. A knock on the door was followed by the sound of breaking glass in the rear of the house. Justin and Diana were not safe. Their grandmother woke them from sleep as she raced to protect them from the intruders. She covered their bodies with her own as the sound of footsteps rapidly ascended the stairs. The door to their room burst open. The children heard a muffled pop and then their grandmother's lifeless body collapsed to the floor in morbid cadence. A single bullet to her head killed her.

A man made a phone call from the phone in the foyer. Other men grabbed the children, covered their mouths, and carried them down the stairs kicking and screaming into the back of a waiting van that blended into the darkness of the night. The motor was running, and the headlights were off. Several cigarettes were on the ground outside the driver's door. A burly man with slicked-back hair was waiting for the children as they exited the house. His tie and jacket seemed out of place. The children were trembling. They had just witnessed the horror of horrors. Diana was sobbing uncontrollably. Justin made his way next to his sister and held her tightly as his mother had done to him on more than one occasion.

The air in the van was dank and dusty. Their captor forced the children to remain on the floor on top of an old mattress. The padded walls muffled their cries. The brakes released, and the van was under way.

Never underestimate the fury of a mother when her children's lives were threatened. Linda didn't remember how she made it onto the highway or to her mother-in-law's house. She gave no thought to her own safety. All she could think about was the scream and unknown assailants terrifying her princess. She had to get there as quickly as she could. What would happen when she arrived crossed her mind only as she turned the corner several blocks before the house. Her teeth were tightly clenched. Her thoughts kept drifting to the unthinkable. What they might do scared her. How could she trust these kidnappers? She needed a plan—and fast. Her cell phone was in her hand. She could always dial 911 and leave the phone on the seat. She knew the police could track the signal and send a patrol car, but the admonition of the voice on the phone echoed in her thoughts: "Inform anyone, your kids die." How could she be sure that they weren't able to monitor her call? She couldn't jeopardize her children's lives, even if it meant putting herself in harm's way.

The morning sun was rising as she turned into her mother-in-law's driveway. The house was in an exclusive community with minimum two-acre plots. Tall oaks and evergreens hid the nearest neighbor from view. An unsettling silence was present. Rage emboldened Linda as she saw the open front door. As she approached, she noted that the doorjamb was shattered. Running, she entered the house shouting, "Diana, Justin, Mom! Where are you?"

Only silence responded. She ran throughout the lower level and then made her way up the stairs. She entered the room at the top of the stairs, and her knees weakened. She fell to the floor, sickened by the sight of blood and half of her mother-in-law's face blown away by the explosive force of the attack.

"Oh dear God!" she screamed.

She was paralyzed by the carnage. She tried to yell for her children, but the tears and tightness in her throat from emotional tension precluded it. Her eyes were focused on an envelope placed on the body. It had her name on it. She reached for it and opened it with some trepidation. She read it aloud as if her mother-in-law were still alive to hear it.

> *We have your children. They will remain alive only if you follow our directions exactly. Your husband has information we need, and this information will be traded for the lives of your children. We will be in touch with you by 6:00 p.m. today to make the trade. If your husband is not present or fails to give us the information we need, your children die. If you go to the authorities, your children die. You now know we will do what we say. We are watching you at all times.*

Linda could no longer contain herself. She held herself tightly, and her sobbing opened the floodgates. Her life was changed at that moment and forever. She knew exactly what she had to do.

39

BREAK-IN

It had been hours since I spoke with Debra at the diner. I was racing home to get Linda and the kids out. I felt I couldn't call. The phones would probably be tapped. Anyway, this was something I had to tell her in person. She had been unbelievably supportive and believing in me. I needed to let her know what I now knew.

I had to be cautious. With all that had occurred over the last two days, I couldn't take any more chances. I needed to pass by my house slowly to make sure no one was there. But if they were there, wouldn't they spot me? I needed a disguise. I remembered the Goodwill drop-off site in the nearby shopping center. We were forever dropping our old clothes off there. It seemed we had a never-ending supply of old clothes. The overflowing bins suggested everyone else did the same.

It took me only a few moments to find a blue peacoat that didn't call attention to itself. It stunk of beer, but I couldn't bother about that right now. It wouldn't look out of place with the jeans and the flannel shirt I was wearing. Remarkably, a blue Michigan Wolverines cap was nearby. I had a flashback to my college days: Saturday afternoons spent with Linda and the fraternity brothers watching with 108,000 others as the Big Blue waged war. These simpler times seemed so long ago. The outfit at least made me inconspicuous, even though I smelled like a drunk.

I turned the corner onto my block. It was early in the afternoon—too soon for the children to be home from school. With mostly professionals living in the neighborhood, the streets were desolate at this time of day with little of the hustle and bustle usually present. I walked past the house from the other side of the street. I kept my head down, buried a bit beneath the collar of the peacoat. I glanced across the street at the house as I passed. My stomach cramped as I saw two figures moving past the windows on the second floor. I kept walking down the block and passed a black Caprice with two big men in the front seats. One was smoking a cigar that had a most acrid odor. The car looked strangely familiar. It wasn't until I passed it that I remembered. It was the same car that was in the marina parking lot that kept inching forward as I moved my boat out. *Dr. Brunswick's henchmen, for sure,* I thought. I also knew what that meant. The men in the house were not invited. I had to know if Linda and the kids were in there.

I rounded the corner and made my way through my neighbor's backyard. I was torn about calling the police. I was likely being sought by now for jumping bail and not showing up for court yesterday. If the police did arrive, my family might be hurt. Anyway, I needed to find out what those people were doing in the house first.

Our modest home had two beautiful and elegant white pillars in the front. However, they paled in comparison to the magnificence of the trees surrounding the house. The grade of the property sloped downward toward the back, creating a two-story colonial from the front and a three-story aboveground structure from the back. A door centered in the back of the house entered the workroom. We kept a well-hidden key to this room on the outside. I was hoping it was still where it should be and that the people inside were still on the upper levels. I was nearing the rear door when I heard voices and then rapid footsteps approaching. I jumped into the shrubs and quickly drew my feet into my chest, hoping to remain hidden. The voices grew louder as they rapidly approached and stopped just feet away from where I lay hidden in the foliage. I could smell the bitter scent of a cigar.

"John, you sure you saw something moving on the side of the house?" the man with the cigar stated with a smoker's raspy voice.

"Could have sworn I did."

"Probably just a raccoon. They're always looking for garbage."

"Maybe, but let's look around, just in case."

They continued their sweep of the area, passing near where I lay frozen in place. I didn't dare breathe for fear of being discovered. They split up and methodically covered the property. They concluded their sweep where it started, only a few short steps from where I was hiding. I dared not move.

"We better get back to the car. The doc's wife should be home real soon. Why don't you give Pat and Jack a call and tell them to finish up," he stated as he continued to puff on his cigar.

I could hear static as the man with the cigar called, not on a cell phone, but rather an old handheld transceiver. "All clear out here. Why don't you finish up and meet us at the car. Over."

The response was not what I expected. I heard a woman's voice over the receiver. "Just collecting the clothes we need for the kids. I already set up the place. We'll be there in five. Over."

"Roger," he stated as he again puffed his cigar.

"Hey, John, you been drinking?" the man with the cigar asked.

"Just the beer at lunch," John responded.

"It smells like a lot more than one beer. You better get rid of that smell before the boss finds out; otherwise, you may not live to spend any of the money," the cigar man stated.

They smelled my coat. Fortunately, they left it at that and didn't pursue it. They moved to the front of the house. I heard car doors close, an engine start, and a car leave. I lifted my head and looked around. It appeared to be all clear. I slowly returned to a seated position. I was hurting from keeping myself in a contorted position, so it took a little time to get myself standing. I needed to get inside before the others left. I wanted to see what they were doing, and more importantly, why. Did they already have my children? I couldn't bear the thought. I found the key just where I had left it under the loose base of the outdoor lighting fixture and entered the workroom. I heard steps from the upstairs. I glanced at the phone and saw a light indicating one of the lines was in use. Should I pick up the receiver? Would they know? I had to. I carefully picked up the receiver, pressed the mute button, and then pressed the lighted line button. They didn't appear to notice. Their conversation continued.

"I got the clothes and set the devices. Couldn't find any legal documents." It was a woman's voice.

The voice on the other end—it was Brunswick! "Damn it, it's there. I know it! We'll just have to have Ludlow assign the rights to us after we do away with Gifford and his family. We just need to make their deaths look like an accident…or better still, an act of desperation by an already accused killer. The beauty of the scheme is that he's already accused of killing Ludlow, who just so happened to have left his financial affairs in the hands of his long-lost brother."

"What makes you think that Ludlow will sign everything over to you?"

"I think he's too scared. He's afraid of what we might do to his wife and the kid we stole for them. He still thinks it was a legal adoption. He believes his long-lost brother."

"Did you move the kids to the lab?" the woman asked.

"Yeah, they're long gone," Brunswick responded.

I had heard enough. If I stayed where I was, I was sure I'd be found out. I made my way back out of the house. Somewhere in my frenzy, the key fell from my pocket. The door locked as I closed it. I made it to the side of the house and started to run. I made it to the sidewalk and then slowed my walk to match the cadence I had before. I didn't look back. I was too fearful of what I might see. A single tear dropped from my eyelid. My God, they had my children.

40

REVELATIONS

Linda was a woman with motivation. Nothing would stop her from trying to save her children, except possibly her death. But that was not an option. She sped toward her house with the words from the letter still echoing in her head. *"If your husband is not present or fails to give us the information we need, your children die. If you go to the authorities, your children die."* She proceeded directly home.

How was she going to find Barry? Without him, how was she going to get the children back? A chilling possibility existed: Would these cold-blooded killers really give them back? Or would they kill them as well as her and her husband? She couldn't let this influence her resolve.

She was several blocks from her house and slowing for a stop sign when the blurred motion of a hooded figure moving through the trees and between yards caught her attention. The falling leaves had left the trees bare, so it was easier to see the blurred figure but still difficult to see clearly. She could just feel that she was being watched. Instead of stopping, she accelerated through the intersection, just missing crossing traffic. Horns blared, and her heart pounded. She looked in her rearview mirror. No one appeared to be following, but that unnerving feeling didn't leave her. She continued several blocks past her house to make sure she wasn't followed before doubling back.

She parked in the garage and closed the garage door behind her. She immediately knew others had been there. Muddy footprints were everywhere. The door leading from the garage to the house was locked. That was very odd; she never left it locked. She also never took a key with her because she was always losing them. Anyway, there was always a spare hidden near the back door, just in case. She exited through the door at the rear of the garage and moved around the back. She kept looking over her shoulder and staying very close to the house. She lifted the loose base of the light fixture next to the back door. The key was gone. A cold breeze blew past her.

Where could it be? she thought. She began looking in the shrubs nearby when she was grabbed from behind. Before she could let out a scream, a hand covered her mouth. Whispering in her ear was a familiar voice. "Linda, it's me."

Her fear quickly turned to relief. Her eyes welled up as she turned to see Barry. Tears began flowing down her cheeks as they embraced. "Barry, I was so worried. I thought I'd never see you again," she said between sobs.

"I know, honey. I still can't believe what's going on," Barry responded.

"They have our children, and they said—" Linda started blurting.

"I know. I overheard a conversation they were having, and I think I know where they're keeping them. We just need to get a few things together first," Barry interrupted.

"And, Barry," her voice lowered as she continued, "they killed your mom."

I was in shock. "Are you sure?" I stated softly.

"Yes, I was there after it happened. They left it as a message," she quietly replied.

I was heartbroken and angry. I wanted revenge. But I didn't want to become Brunswick. Linda knew what to say to snap me out of it. I would need to deal with these emotions later.

"But, Barry, we don't have time." Linda's face tensed, and her voiced sharpened. "They gave me until six o'clock; otherwise, they'll kill our children."

“They won’t do that. They need me. That is, they need me dead. I’m the only one who can stop them, and that’s exactly what I plan to do!” I stated defiantly.

“How can you be so sure? How can you be willing to bet the lives of our children?” Linda replied.

“Let’s get inside, and I’ll explain. Damn, where is that key?” I patted himself down looking for the key. Linda was searching between bushes. “I know I had it. Can’t waste the time looking.” I broke a pane of glass in the back door with my elbow and reached inside to open the door. As we entered the house, Linda walked slowly and stopped often.

“I feel so violated, Barry…and so scared. I don’t feel like this is our house. I used to feel so secure inside. Now I feel that I’m exposed and vulnerable and can’t do anything about it.”

“I know where you’re coming from, but you’ve got to believe me—we will get our lives back, and we will get our children back. Those who have attacked us and our children will not win. Let me tell you what I know so far.”

I sat on the sofa and held Linda in my arms. Then I started to tell the story, beginning with the courthouse, the diatribe by Brunswick, how he thought I was his brother, and ending with overhearing the conversation on the phone between the woman and Dr. Brunswick.

However, I knew there were pieces missing. I now knew why they attacked me in the parking lot. But why did they take the risk of setting me up for the murder of a person who was still alive? And why wasn’t I dead? They sure had enough opportunity. Were they just incompetent, or was it that they still needed me alive? Then it all started making sense.

“Linda, do you remember when we first spoke about getting married? I told you how I became interested in fertility.”

“Of course. You were concerned about something your father had told you about an illness you had as a child and that there might be a problem having children of your own.”

“And?”

"Well, you just wanted me to know, just in case that made a difference to me. And it didn't, and we didn't have any difficulty having children."

"That's exactly as I had told you, but my dad said something else too. Something that didn't make sense at the time. I seem to remember my dad telling me about a family curse. His estranged brother had a defective gene that was passed to his children. My dad lost all contact with his brother after his brother's wife died during childbirth. It was rumored that she gave birth to triplets, and only one of the triplets reportedly survived. He mentioned one other thing that didn't have any meaning at the time. That my dad's brother used to take trips abroad for hunting. That story is similar to what Brunswick retold. What if the rumor was wrong? What if the other two babies survived?"

"Barry, what does that mean? What are you getting at?"

"Well, when I was in Dr. Brunswick's boardroom, he said that he was one of three siblings, and two of the children had been given up for adoption at birth. He also said that his father was a hunter, Bob was his brother, and his mother died in childbirth."

"Couldn't this all be a coincidence?" Linda questioned.

"I'm sure it isn't," I responded. "He called me his brother. What does he know that I don't? What if Brunswick was right? I was the third child and adopted by my parents. What if I carry the genetic answer that he is searching for?"

"I still don't understand," Linda said. "What does he want from you?"

"I think he feels there is something in my genetics that is the key to his research. Something so important he will kill to get it. I believe it all goes back to the assault in the parking lot outside my office. His intent was to get the data on my research that had just been delivered. My wrist was injured when they took my watch and exchanged it for the fake. I never really figured out why they did this. I was also left with a deep abrasion on my hip. Which I now know was to get a sample for genetic testing. That's it!" I yelled, surprising Linda.

"What, Barry? What is 'it'?"

"Linda, we need to get up to the attic. I think the answers and the way to save our children is in that old trunk of my dad's."

41

FAMILY SECRETS

The attic was dark and dusty. We rarely went up there. We'd lived in the house for ten years and might have ventured into the attic half a dozen times. I had been meaning to get up there to clean the place but just never had the time.

My dad was a genealogy buff. He would spend hours on the weekend researching the family tree. He had a trunk where he stored his findings—such diverse things as clippings from newspaper articles to gravestone rubbings to reams of notes he had collected over the years. Unfortunately, his many years of smoking and business pressure took its toll. The trunk had been in our attic since we moved him to a skilled nursing facility following his stroke. He died several years ago.

"Linda, when I was attacked in the parking lot, I believe it was for more than to get my notes on my research. They used the mugging as a cover for their real purpose: to take samples from me for genetic testing."

"What?" Linda blurted incredulously.

"I couldn't figure out at the time why my wrist, hip, and back were hurting as much as my head and why I was black and blue in these areas. Now I know they pulled my watch off to exchange it with the duplicate and then used it to frame me. The frame was to keep me occupied while they ran the tests and get the media to think it was their data while I was being investigated. They staged Bob's death and knew that I would be released once he reappeared. I also believe they took skin, blood, and likely bone marrow samples from me for analysis. That would explain the persistent aching pain and discolored areas that lasted so long."

"Why would they do that? It sounds perverted."

"He thinks I am his brother. He said that in the boardroom at ReproMed. I think they suspected my DNA might hold the key. We had no difficulty having children, and that sparked their interest. The work I was doing with Bob had indicated that the gene was dominant and attached to the X chromosome. That meant it could be passed only from the mother and not the father to each male offspring. However, the substance we isolated didn't work in all animals we had tested it in. We suspected a protective genetic factor—possibly something on the gene that affected its action—was present in some of these animals. This is probably what they learned from my research. If this were true for humans, then the fact that I was not affected would mean I had the protective genetic factor." I took a breath.

"It would be a simple test to compare the gene map of my Y chromosome to that of Dr. Brunswick's and Bob's variant gene attached to their X chromosome. But they needed my genetic material to analyze. What was missing on theirs and present on mine would indicate the likely site of damage. They would therefore know exactly which area of the Y chromosome needed to be blocked to stop sperm production.

"However, what they failed to consider was that there could also be another reason why my Y chromosome was normal. Simply that we did not share the same mother. They suspected me because I shared a particular gene mutation that he and I suspect Bob also had. They were so engrossed in their corrupt plot, they failed even to entertain the possibility that I was not the third baby born to their mother. They were too concerned that I would figure it out. They had to get me out of the lab. What better way than to have me imprisoned by framing me for Bob's murder? But why Bob was part of this I still don't understand."

"What does the trunk have to do with all this?" Linda asked.

I didn't answer right away. I really didn't know what I would find.

"I believe Dr. Brunswick is holding our children as more than just hostages. He believes Justin, in particular, carries the protective gene, just like he thinks I do. As long as he believes this, he'll let them live," I stated.

"I don't think he reviewed my genetic report in its entirety," I continued. "I believe he would have found that I'm not a genetic progeny of his mother."

"How can you be so sure?" Linda asked.

"Because Bob, and I suspect Brunswick, don't have an intact Y chromosome. They have only two X chromosomes, so they cannot obtain information about paternal ancestry. It is the mitochondrial DNA they needed to compare. Mitochondrial DNA comes only from the mother and would provide confirmation of maternal ancestry. I'm not exactly sure what I'll find in the trunk, but I know the answer lies in my family's past."

The trunk was covered with a thick layer of dust. The front was locked, and no key was in sight. I found an old screwdriver lying nearby and used it to pry open the lock. The cover of the trunk creaked as it opened. The smell was that of age…with a faint pungent smell that I couldn't identify. Lying on top was a picture of my mom and dad framed in a tarnished silver frame. They appeared to be in their twenties. Young and in love. Mom was so beautiful, but her face was fuller and her body heavier then I remembered.

We kept searching through the trunk, not exactly sure what we were looking for. The picture of my parents kept popping back in my mind. Something about that picture seemed unusual, but I couldn't put my finger on it: their happiness, my mom's weight, or my mom's belly? Was she pregnant? It would be several years before I was born. Did I have a sibling? My dad always told me they had waited so long to have children because they felt it was important to invite your children into this world when you were truly emotionally and financially able to undertake this responsibility.

Near the bottom of the trunk, we came across a nondescript folder. Upon opening it, we found two items: a gravestone rubbing and a thick envelope. The gravestone rubbing was on inexpensive paper. The edges were burned with age and the tracing was disappearing. It was a simple memorial to a departed loved one. Both Linda and I read the inscription at the same time.

"Our beloved son, Bernard Justin Gifford, born April 20, 1952. Died April 21, 1952." We looked at each other in disbelief.

I had a brother. Why did he die? Was it a genetic disease? I took the unopened envelope. It had the imprint of a prestigious law firm in town. Inside I found legal papers. The cover page was titled "Trust for Benefit of Dexter Brunswick and Kevin O'Brien, amended January 7, 1985."

42

SWITCHBACK

We continued to read the trust document. The governor had left sizable assets for these deserted offspring. Whether it be guilt or remorse, he set up trusts to assure financial security for these abandoned children. He also knew their names. He referred to a private adoption for Kevin O'Brien and enclosed a birth certificate for Dexter Brunswick. The document also listed his brother, my father, as a trustee. There was also an article in the manila folder titled "Orphanage Director Found Guilty of Embezzlement."

I now knew who my uncle was and that both Bob and Brunswick were my cousins. What really shocked me at first was that Detective Kevin O'Brien was also my cousin. But then it made sense. He knew. His interview with me was a ruse. He was watching over me the whole time. I wondered if Bob and he were working in concert. That would certainly make more sense than Bob being Brunswick's pawn. I could only hope that was so.

You take your roots for granted. To find out that I had cousins—and three cousins at that—was unsettling. Why would my father keep this from me? Why would he not let me know I had cousins? The only thing I knew was that he had a falling-out with his brother early in life over a business deal gone bad. He never had contact with him afterward. The fact that his brother's children and I were born on the same day was eerie. The only thing that made sense was that my father didn't know. The envelope was unopened. It was probably received after he passed.

"Barry, are you all right?" Linda asked softly.

"I'm just a little stunned by finding the trust document. I just found out that I have three cousins that I have been interacting with but never knew. And at least one is trying to kill me and my family. It's almost as if I had a bad dream and want to wake up so it'll go away. I know I'm no different than I was minutes before finding these papers. I just can't shake it.

"Wait a minute. Dr. Brunswick's people never found these papers. He doesn't know that I am not a full sibling of his. That's why Brunswick's experiments haven't worked. He used my Y chromosomal structure as a template to compare with his and Bob's Y chromosome fragments, thinking that differences would be indicative of regions responsible for sperm production. He doesn't know I'm not related through maternal DNA. He made genetic segments that likely have no relationship to sperm production, and he doesn't know why it doesn't work in his human tests. It probably just elevates testosterone, resulting in excessive production of red blood cells. That's why these young men are dying from strokes. He can't figure it out. He needs me. At least he thinks he needs me. Linda, we're not going to be victims anymore. We're going to turn the tables on Dr. Brunswick. What time do you have?"

"Five fifty-five. We have ten minutes until they said they'd make contact," Linda replied.

"I'm counting on it." Well, maybe I wasn't so positive, but I was hoping they would call it. We could then use the displayed number they called from to locate them. I was hoping it would be a number I knew.

I needed a few things first. They would try to use the kids as bait and then as hostages. We needed the element of surprise—and a backup. We needed to get them off balance and feeling a little unsure of themselves.

Linda went to grab a few things the children would need: food, clothes, and some toys to keep them occupied. I went down to the den where I kept my safe. I needed to make sure I was armed. Linda never liked me having guns. I never thought I'd be carrying one; that's for sure. I got hooked on the sport in college and just kept it up afterward. But when my children's lives were at stake, I wasn't going to take a chance.

I unlocked the safe and took out the Kahr 9 mm. It was small enough to put in my pants pocket. I inserted the magazine, unlocked the external safety, and put another loaded magazine in my pocket. I locked the safe. Things seemed surreal.

I could hear Linda's phone ring. I called out to her. "Don't answer it yet! See if a number is shown on the screen."

"Barry, I don't know the number. It's 625-7756. Do you know it?"

"I sure do. You can answer the call now."

I knew that number only too well. They were calling from the lab at ReproMed. Matt Dean always gave me that number. I thought it was his private number since he personally answered on the first or second ring.

I was sitting on the couch next to Linda as she answered the phone. Her brow was furrowed, and her complexion was pale. I hoped she could keep it together long enough. She lived and breathed for the children. Just the presence of a cold would make her stay up at night tiptoeing into their rooms to make sure they were comfortable and not in distress. The stress must have been as unbearable for her as it was for me. Linda switched to her cell phone's speakerphone.

I could not place the female voice on the phone as I started to hear the conversation.

"The children are safe and crying for you." Tears were coming to Linda's eyes as the voice continued, "If you follow my directions, no harm will come to them. But if you don't, you will get them back in pieces." With that Linda was about to come apart. I had to cover her mouth to prevent her verbally assailing the thug.

I took the phone and took it off the speakerphone. I did not want to traumatize Linda anymore. I also knew I had to be very careful of what I said. I needed them to think we would do everything that was asked yet also plant a seed of concern. I did not want Linda to interject with emotional outbursts. "Who is this?" I demanded.

"Dr. Gifford. You have eluded us. Congratulations! However, I believe we have something that you would like returned. Wouldn't you agree?" the male voice stated with a clear tone of superiority.

I still couldn't place the voice. It sounded somewhat familiar. "If you're referring to our children, we expect that no harm will come to them. What do you want from us?" I tried to sound angry yet concerned.

"Upset, are you? Well, that's good. Just remember your kids' survival is in your hands. Just do as you're told, and you'll be with them soon."

I felt like reaching through the phone and pulling his heart out. The bastard. I had to keep my cool. I had to remain in control and not let him manipulate the situation, but I also needed to let him think he controlled me. "You hurt them, and I'll not stop till you're dead."

"Dr. Gifford, don't get so testy. We want you and your wife to drive to Canyon Road. There's a gas station on the northwest corner. Wait there until you see a green pickup truck. The driver will flash the headlights. That will be the sign for you to follow. Any sign of the police or other cars, and you'll regret it. Be there precisely at seven o'clock."

"Seven o'clock? It's at least an hour's drive from here."

"Then you better get started, Dr. Gifford." The line went dead.

I hung up the phone. Linda was breathing rapidly. She said she was feeling lightheaded. I had her lie down. "Honey, they want us to meet them at Canyon Road where a truck will meet us and presumably lead us to see the children. And they want us there in one hour."

"One hour!" Linda exclaimed.

"I know it takes almost that time to get there. That's why we're going to where the phone call was made. Matt Dean's office. I think we'll find the children there. No, I'm sure we'll find the children there." I didn't tell her that the children might not be all we would find.

Linda tearfully responded. "But they'll kill the children! We must follow their instructions."

"No, they won't. They need them to get what they think they need from me. They know that if anything happens to them, they'll never get it. I need to get to ReproMed. That's where they have our children."

"No, Barry. They'll kill you and the children."

"They may try. That's why we'll need help. It is time to get my cousin, Detective O'Brien, involved. He is in the One Hundred Sixth Precinct. You need to call him and tell him Bob's alive, that they are holding our children at ReproMed, and that I'm on the way. He'll know what to do. And as a diversion, call the One Hundred Sixth Precinct, which is near to Brunswick's office, to report a break-in at his office. That should get the help we need and hopefully keep Brunswick far away from the lab."

"Barry, what are you going to do? Why don't you just wait for the police to arrive to rescue them?"

"Because there's someone on the force working for Dr. Brunswick. How else could they arrest me without a shred of credible evidence? I need to find the proof, which I'm sure is in the lab, before Brunswick finds out that I'm his cousin and not his brother. We would then become a liability. He would kill all of us to cover his tracks. The only way we have a chance is to prove their guilt...I'm sure the proof is in the lab."

43

DUPLICITY

I didn't want to leave Linda, but I knew I had to. I had to keep her a safe distance away. If anything happened to me, I didn't want her to be hurt. Besides, she was one of the few I could trust with my life. I took a cab to ReproMed and asked to be dropped a block away.

It was dark when I reached ReproMed. Only a few lights were visible on the tenth floor. Matt Dean's office was on the tenth floor. I could see only one security guard in the front lobby. This posed a problem. I certainly didn't want them to know I was coming.

I entered through the parking garage under the building. A black Mercedes was waiting for the attendant. A very tall woman with jet-black hair was standing next to the car. I couldn't help but notice the bright-red key case she passed to the parking attendant. Her overcoat seemed out of place. It was bulky and not in keeping with her elegant appearance. The parking attendant drove off to park her car. I approached the young woman at the elevator.

"Excuse me, can I get to Matt Dean's office from these elevators?"

"Sure can," she responded. Obviously, she knew who Matt Dean was. "He's on the tenth floor, room ten-ten right down the hall from my office. I don't know if he's here at this hour, but I'd be happy to show you the way." Her voice sounded familiar.

"I'd appreciate that," I said, waiting for the follow-up question that was sure to follow.

"I haven't seen him all day. I hope he knows you're coming." Somehow, I think she knew the real answer.

I tried to sound as truthful as I could, given the circumstances. "He had called and asked me to come right over. He said something about this project he was working on that needed my attention right away. I just got into town and didn't even have the opportunity to change."

"Sounds just like Matt. He's been working late hours over the past several weeks and always with urgent problems needing immediate attention. I've gotten calls like that myself. Where are you from?"

I had to think fast. I remembered Matt had mentioned a Dr. Taylor from England who was coming by to assist him on a research project several weeks ago. "England. I work with Dr. Taylor. Maybe you know him."

"Can't say I do. But there are always visitors from overseas. Well, welcome to ReproMed."

I proceeded toward the elevators with the young woman as my guide. We passed the security booth, and she smiled and waved to the security guard. He obviously knew the young woman I had befriended. I was glad I did. The guard must have thought I was with her. I glanced at the card she carried around her neck. Her badge indicated she was a senior research associate. She pressed the elevator button.

"Couldn't help noticing that you work in research. Are you involved with any of Matt's research?" I asked. Her voice continued sounding familiar.

"No, not me. He works directly with Dr. Brunswick. All very secretive. That's probably why you've been called in so urgently. The project has hit a major snag that needs to be fixed by week's end; otherwise, they stand to lose their investors' backing. That would mean a lot of us would be out of a job. It's been pretty frenetic up on the tenth as of late," she stated.

That explained the need for creating such a diversion. Dr. Brunswick needed a week to present his data to his investors. He must have known I was on the verge of publishing my work. He couldn't afford to have me do that, especially when the unfortunate subjects he tried his recombinant product on had significant side effects. The elevator door opened. We both stepped in. What luck! She placed her key in the slot next to floor ten and turned it. The doors closed, and the elevator started upward.

I needed to get into the lab. If my children were there, they would be tightly guarded. Maybe I could ease my access into the lab by enlisting the help of my newfound friend. I held the door to the elevator open as she exited. "Would you mind directing me to Matt Dean's office?"

"It would be my pleasure," she immediately responded, almost as if she had anticipated my question. "It's right down the hall on the left. I believe his door is open. Follow me. I'm headed that way."

It was all going too smoothly. Maybe that's what made me suspicious. I reached my hand into my pocket and made sure the gun was still there. I was feeling flushed, and my hand started shaking. We approached the open door. I cautiously approached and looked inside, not anticipating what would occur next.

"This is the place, Dr. Gifford," she stated as I recognized her voice from the phone call. She was the one who brought me here. She somehow knew I would know where the call originated. She never left the building. She was waiting in the garage for me to come.

When I heard my name, I knew immediately I had fallen into a trap. I saw in the reflection of the chrome doorjamb that my elevator companion was brandishing a gun of her own, and it was aimed directly at me. I wasn't going to be stopped now, not with my children's lives at stake.

Without hesitation, I turned into her with my left elbow landing squarely on the side of her head. The blow knocked her off her feet. Her gun went flying out of her hand, and her head made contact with the wall. Blood splattered over the wall as she collapsed in a limp heap on the floor. I stood there for a moment in shock. I couldn't believe I did that…and to a woman. And me, a physician, dedicated to saving lives, and I had possibly taken a second life. But that brief interlude was broken with the reality of my children being threatened by these thugs. The noise had to catch the attention of others. I thought all hell was going to break loose. My gun was already out of my pocket and readied. I stood in the hallway just outside the open door.

I heard Diana's words between her sobs. "You're not going to…be so happy when my daddy gets here. He's going to hurt you."

They hadn't heard me yet.

"Your daddy will be up here soon, and when he does arrive, I'll be very happy." This gruff voice spoke with obvious satisfaction. "Get the children to the back room. I'll close the front door."

It didn't seem like they heard the commotion in the hallway. I had to make my move now while I still had the element of surprise. I stayed low and crawled into the room, keeping to the side of the file cabinets. I recognized the goon who came to close the front door as the driver of the car that was outside my house. I seized the opportunity as he came to the front door.

I picked up a floor lamp next to the desk. He heard the noise and turned. The lamp was already in motion, and it caught him on the side of his head. His surprised expression turned into one of contorted confusion. I stood there a moment too long and felt a whoosh of air as he grabbed my left arm, pulling it forward. He plummeted to the floor, unconscious. Searing pain followed tearing flesh. I readied my gun, anticipating what was to come. I dived to the floor just in front of the desk. The second goon was rushing from the back room to finish me off. He appeared around the corner of the desk, ready to fire. He didn't expect to be greeted by a 9 mm slug. It hit him squarely in the chest, freezing his forward motion. He grasped his chest as he fell. I got to my feet and ran to the children. My left arm felt useless. I was surprised at the lack of pain.

I found the children huddled together behind a couch in the inner room that served as a waiting area for visitors to the lab. I couldn't contain myself. The gun slipped from my grip, and I grabbed them and hugged them with my good arm. I didn't want to let go, but I had to get them out of here. I hoped the police arrive soon. A voice drew my attention. It was the goon I had landed with the lamp. He was only stunned. This time he had recovered his gun.

"Dr. Gifford. Too bad. You almost made it." He raised his gun and took aim.

"Don't do that," a familiar voice commanded from the side.

"Mr. Ludlow, my orders were to kill them—all of them."

"Well, I'm changing your orders. There will be no more killing. There shouldn't have been any." The tightness in Bob's throat punctuated his words.

"Sorry, that's what Dr. Brunswick said you might say."

A rally of gunfire followed. The goon was hit twice by bullets from a gun that appeared in Bob's hand. It was as if it was happening in slow motion. I saw Bob falling, and I rushed to his side.

He was hit in the chest and left side of his neck. I immediately applied pressure to the carotid artery, knowing full well it was only a temporary measure. "Bob, why?" I asked, not knowing what the response would be.

"Barry, I never thought it would go this far," he stated with a weak voice as he gulped for air. Life was draining from his body. "No one was supposed to get hurt. I loved my wife so much, and he was family. A brother I never knew, but ill and in need of my help. And you, a lost cousin I respected and the focus of my brother's criminal intentions. Detective O'Brien, my other brother and your cousin, found out about us. He was concerned about your safety and enjoined me to help protect you. Debra wanted a child more than anything. I didn't know how insane my brother was until it was too late. He used drugs to control me. I couldn't let them hurt you or your family.

"Please tell Debra I love her…more than life itself."

The words ended as the last of the air left his lungs.

44

INJUSTICE

The children were safe for now. I knew the police would be here soon. Linda would make sure of that. I wouldn't let the police near the children. I didn't know whom I could trust. Police! That was what these goons reminded me of. The way they searched my house. Very methodically yet curiously restoring everything they had moved back to its original position. Just like Larry described what happened at the annex of the courthouse after Michael Silva was shot. There was a reason they brought the children here. I needed to find out why.

A bright-green light was emanating from under a blue door on my way to the elevator. The children were clinging to me, sobbing uncontrollably. I walked with them out of Matt Dean's office and toward the elevator. Halfway down the hallway was where the green light was coming from. "Day Care Center" was printed in block letters on the door. I wondered why a scientific facility would have a day care center, especially one on the tenth floor down the hallway from the main laboratory.

I tried the doorknob. The door was unlocked. I found the light switch and turned the lights on. I entered with the children close in tow. I wasn't quite prepared for what I found: a classroom of soundproof booths with computer terminals at each. A green light was glowing at the front of the room. I could hear a faint sound from the booth I was near. I picked up the set of headphones lying on the desk. It was Dr. Brunswick's voice I heard. I listened long enough to know what this day care center really was.

I looked back as we were about to enter the elevator. The bodies were sprawled over the room like a war zone. The woman masquerading as an employee was lying in a pool of blood by the office door. One of the men lay just inside the door with a hand outstretched. The gun lying near his hand after I caught him with the base of the lamp. I kicked the gun far away, just in case. The other goon was facedown, head to the side, eyes wide open, and life long gone. And then there was poor Bob on his side. Was that breathing motion I detected? I ran to his side. The children stayed together near the elevator door. I could feel a faint brachial pulse.

"Bob, are you with me?" I whispered as I knelt at his side.

"Barry, you must stop him. You know the enemy of whom I speak."

The enemy of whom I speak? That was in the letter slid under my door—the letter that *Bob* slid under my door. "Bob, why? Why did you betray our friendship?"

"I didn't betray our friendship. I was protecting you and your family. At least I thought I was. He stole your ideas and claimed them for his own. I couldn't stand for that. But that wasn't all. He was brilliant for sure but also very sick. He would find unsuspecting patients and then treat them with his recombinant product without even testing it on animals first. He wanted to create a society of sterile clones. That was his way to get back at the society he hated for shutting him out."

Bob was dying. I needed to get help for him—and quickly. I called 911 on my cell phone and gave them the location. They would be here soon. I had to get my children out of here. That was my mission now. I didn't know if any of Dr. Brunswick's men were still around.

I left ReproMed with the children's hands inextricably locked into mine. The pain in my arm was assuaged by the joy of holding my children. I could not stop my teeth from grinding. I can't remember feeling so much hatred directed toward a single individual. My children were traumatized, and their scars would be with them throughout their lives. My mother was killed, and my career was on the verge of imploding, and all for what? Dr. Brunswick's lust for revenge.

We exited through the garage. It was a bit odd that the attendant was nowhere to be found. I reached into the attendant's office and took the bright-red key case for the Mercedes that was parked in front of the office. I knew the driver wouldn't be needing it anymore. I certainly wasn't going to wait to see if anyone else was around.

I secured Diana and Justin into the rear seats. They were still trembling as we left the garage. Looking back at the building through my rearview mirror, I could see the police cars and emergency vehicles surrounding the front of the building. I caught a glimpse of the figure of a man leaving through the side of the building. I knew who he was. I didn't have time to stop and take care of unfinished business. I needed to get the children to safety first. I knew where he was going.

45

RETRIBUTION

Linda couldn't control her tears at the sight of the children. They had sobbed for most of the trip back to our house, and then the sight of their mother brought loud crying. The catharsis was needed. I hoped Bob would be found alive and could be saved. Though his betrayal was still difficult for me to agree with, his motives were honorable. I just wished he could have handled it a different way.

With the children secure with their mother, I needed to finish what I had started. Dr. Brunswick was on his way to my lab—he had to be with ReproMed in shambles and the police swarming the place. At least those police he hadn't bought. He needed to secure my notes and sequencer data. That way, I wouldn't have any credible evidence to support my story. That's probably why he wanted me to go to a remote location to pick up the children. It would give him and his men time to pilfer my lab. He hadn't been expecting me to show up at ReproMed. He was alone—and that made him vulnerable.

I hadn't been back to University Hospital since this whole thing began. My suspended privileges meant my security card access to the research building was also suspended. The research building was a free-standing structure built several years ago. It was to be the crowning touch to the development of the hospital as a true "university" hospital. We had signed an agreement with City University a decade ago to train their medical students, and in return, they gave us the rights to use their name in our advertising. That was a tremendous draw for our hospital and created such a surge in referrals that over the past decade, the hospital had expanded twice.

The research wing was built almost as an afterthought. The change in health-care reimbursement created a need to generate additional income, and only the pharmaceutical giants had the money. That's when some savvy administrator suggested building a dedicated research facility. It was an instant success, bringing in millions of dollars a year in both basic science grants and clinical research. A walkway was built between the fourth floors of the department of medicine and the research building. A few of the physicians with strong research backgrounds applied for grant money. Those who were awarded grants were given laboratory space. That was how I ended up with a lab. My grant funded support for the staff.

I knew if I entered through the main lobby, I would be able to take the elevator to the fourth floor and make my way to the walkway going to the research building. It was night, and I was sure there would be limited security. I knew most of the guards by name, and they knew me. Not exactly a way to keep my arrival a secret. I knew, though, if I could catch Dr. Brunswick in the act, I could use the security staff to support me.

I parked in visitors' parking and walked cautiously into the hospital lobby. There was a new guard at the desk. He didn't even look up from his paper. I supposed he wouldn't be employed long, but it worked for me. There was very little activity in the lobby. The usual bustle present during the day was replaced by the calm serenity of the night. I made it to the bank of elevators without being noticed. As I entered the elevator and pushed the button for the fourth floor, it seemed all too familiar. The familiar scents of a hospital were not soon forgotten.

I exited on the fourth floor and made my way to corridor C, where the walkway entrance would be. I heard voices ahead and stopped, immediately looking for some type of cover. I found the janitor's closet door ajar and quickly went in. It was a large closet with shelves of supplies. I left the door slightly open, so I could see what transpired. The voices were approaching. I couldn't yet make out what they were discussing. Then I heard my name.

"Can't let Dr. Gifford by," Brunswick declared.

"Why is that, Dr. Brunswick?" the guard asked.

"He's wanted by the police. Something to do with a murder. They consider him armed and dangerous," Brunswick responded.

"Why would you think he would come here?" the guard inquired.

"I'm not sure. I think he might have something important hidden in his laboratory. That's why I called the police. They said a Detective Tollins is on the way. Please make sure he's shown the way to the lab," Brunswick stated.

So that was how he did it. Detective Tollins was the one who arrested me and was likely on Dr. Brunswick's payroll. The security guard left via the stairs, probably to go to the lobby to meet Detective Tollins. The opportunity was now. I had to corner Dr. Brunswick before he got to my laboratory.

I saw him turn and head to the walkway. I started to make my move, opening the closet door. I heard a sound behind me and turned to look. It was Detective Tollins, hiding in the closet with me. Dr. Brunswick, hearing the commotion, opened the door as Tollins held me.

Tollins patted me down. He took the gun from my pocket and handed it to Brunswick. They dragged me to my laboratory where they bound me to a chair. Dr. Brunswick took my gun, held it up to Tollins's head, and shot him. Dr. Brunswick stood in front of me, straddling a chair.

"Well, brother, too bad you killed Detective Tollins. He was the one person who could support your alibi," Dr. Brunswick stated with a smirk.

"You're deeply troubled, Brunswick! You need help. All the killings, all the pain, and for what? Money, power, prestige? You'll have none of that once they find you." I needed to keep him occupied since I didn't know what he had in store for me. I needed time to figure out what his devious mind was thinking and how I could end his reign of terror.

"You insolent bastard. I've followed your career for years. I knew you would be great. Well, hell, now I know why! We share the same genes. I've even supported your research. Who do you think donated the money for the sequencer? I hated you for your ability to be loved and have children—something I could never have. It wasn't fair, and if I couldn't have it, I would make sure no one could. Then I would have control…I would be a god."

He was certainly insane, but I still needed to know his plans. I needed to keep him thinking there was something he needed from me. "How do you think you're going make it out of here? Kill me, and they'll find out about you. Your empire is in ruins, and your ideas are based on erroneous data." I waited for his response.

"I don't need any of them. They are leeches, just in it for the money. They don't understand the science. And you? You think you're smarter than I am? What do you think you know? Bob thought he could outsmart me, and look where he ended up."

It was my opportunity. "You thought by comparing Bob's and my DNA you could identify the factor responsible for suppressing sperm production. You took tissue from Bob in a sham procedure and blood from me when you had your crew attack me in the parking lot outside my office. But you failed to know one very significant factor." I waited for his response before continuing.

"What very significant factor do you think you know?" he asked with a somewhat concerned affect.

"That I am not your brother but rather your cousin."

I saw that my revelation clearly surprised him, but he didn't quite believe it.

"Yeah, right, and I'm supposed to believe you?" he queried.

"I do have an addendum to a trust document from your biological father that tells it all," I said with clear defiance. I could see he was agitated. "But I think you know that already. Why else were your goons at my house? You knew there was something missing. They failed to find the old trunk in the attic. They failed to find the death certificate of Bernard Justin Gifford, my brother who died a day after he was born, and they failed to find a trust listing my father, your uncle, as trustee. That's right. Your work was flawed. We had different parents. My genetics only contaminated your work."

Dr. Brunswick was clearly in shock. He stumbled backward, regained his balance, and lunged for me with his hands readied to grab my neck and choke me. Pushing my feet to the floor, I could stand and bend at the waist with the chair still tied to me. I turned my head away from his advance and caught his gut with the legs of the chair. I heard a cracking sound. The chair leg must have caught a rib. The chair leg also loosened with the impact. I continued to turn and broke the chair on the wall. I was free. I turned, expecting to find Dr. Brunswick on the floor, but there he was, holding a gun pointed at me. I froze in place.

This was it, I thought. I heard a gunshot. I didn't feel the bullet. Was this the way it was when you died? Then I looked down to find Dexter Brunswick lying on the floor in a pool of blood. There at the door was Detective O'Brien, a 9 mm Glock in his hand with smoke emanating from the freshly fired chamber.

ABOUT THE AUTHOR

Bruce R. Gilbert MD, PhD, drew on his long career in medicine for inspiration when writing his new thriller. Gilbert, a graduate of the Weill Cornell School of Medicine, is a Professor of Urology and Director of Male Reproductive and Sexual Medicine at the Zucker School of Medicine at Hofstra/Northwell. He is also an adjunct Clinical Professor of Urology and Reproductive Medicine at Weill Cornell Medical College.

Gilbert also serves as the Medical Director of New York Cryo a Reproductive Tissue Bank and President of Genecord, an umbilical stem cell bank.

He has authored three medical textbooks and over one hundred scientific papers. He lives in New York with his wife Betsy and dog Callie.

Visit his website at www.BruceRGilbert.com